Codename:Hotel

The story of a soldier...
and the woman who tried to save him.

David Travelyan

Prologue

It was not just female intuition. It was not second guessing. She called it 'the waves', a description her girlfriends found easy to understand. She was to discover, years after the date of the events depicted here, from so-called experts in the field, that it was a *'demonstration of a paranormal event, or series of events, exhibiting apparent communication from one mind to another of thoughts, feelings, desires etc. involving mechanisms that cannot be understood in terms of known scientific laws'*
Colonel Sir Charles Crayne, her father, had thought it was 'all hocus pocus'. It took a while for him to accept that there was such a phenomenon as paranormal communication. After he had agreed that it was possible, given that men sometimes had 'hunches' and women sometimes had a 'sixth sense', it was only a small step for him to appreciate that some would be more copiously endowed than others, as is the case with all human beings. Finally, he had to accept that his daughter was one of those supremely blessed with the gift. Or, was she cursed?

Codename:Hotel

Part One

Chapter One
02.30hours 6th June 1944 Bishop's Lodge

Charlotte Crayne woke suddenly. The general chaos of the bedsheets, and the trickle of perspiration running down her back, testified to the discomfort of her sleep over the last few minutes. She looked anxiously around the room, hoping to find a cause for her concern. Perhaps some rodent from the extensive fields around the house had gained access to the premises and caused some small noise that had alarmed her. She sat still and silent, but heard no scurrying, no scratching. Slipping on her dressing gown, she quietly left the bedroom to investigate the possibility that there was some disturbance from downstairs. The nightlight that her father liked to keep in the hall was burning dimly, with steady, uninterrupted flame. As she entered the kitchen, Barney, the Great Dane which had been the family pet for as long as she could remember, raised his head and studied her quizzically. Returning to her bedroom, having found no explanation for her agitated condition, she had to face the hideous truth. Lieutenant James Courtney, her fiance, the man she loved, was in imminent and mortal danger.

Foin, a town of Northern France, near Calais. 02.00 6th June 1944

Lieutenant James Courtney crashed over a small clump of grass growing out of the sand-dunes which were a feature of this area. The unconscious body of his friend, Henri Lebel, landed heavily on top of him. Exhausted and winded James certainly did not need the further complication which now presented itself. As if the mission had not gone badly enough, to find a German soldier sitting here, at the exact location where he was due to be recovered by one of SOE's dedicated high speed craft, was, he felt, beyond a coincidence. So far past the rendezvous time had he arrived here that he would be lucky if the craft were still in the area. His heart leapt when, gazing into the pitch black of the English Channel, he saw the two brief green flashes which were the sign that his rescuers were nearby. His one piece of luck was that his own flashlight was still working. Two flashes would bring the boat to the shore so that he could be ex-filtrated. First, however, he would have to deal with the German, and there was very little time.

Leaving Henri where he was, James stood up and adopted what he hoped was a casual manner. Indeed, it would be unusual for a German sentry to encounter a French peasant, which was the disguise James had adopted for this mission, at this time of night, in this particular location, but the main thing was to keep the initiative, and not put the sentry on his guard. The German was sitting on an upturned barrel, apparently looking at a photograph; his wife? Or maybe a sweetheart? No matter; James had a job to do and do it he must. It was important for

James to get as close as possible, but also to give away his presence before being noticed, so that there would be no indication that he was creeping up on the man. Silently, James approached his adversary, who looked fit and well made. After a few paces, when he was as close as he dared approach and with the tension mounting, James called out, in fluent French, "Excuse me Sir, I have been injured and I am lost. Can you help me?"

"Why have you ignored the curfew?" replied the German in aggressive tone.

"Pardon?" replied James, a ruse to get closer to the man before he launched what would have to be a murderous attack. The German stood up, and, to James' great relief, took a few paces toward him, thereby bringing himself within attacking distance.

"I said why have..." the last sound was muffled by James' forearm smashing into the German's face. He fell heavily, but soon regained his feet. James was at him immediately, landing a punch with sickening power into the man's solar plexus. This should have finished the affair, but this man must have been very fit and tenacious, as he lashed out with his foot, dealing James an agonizing blow to the shin. James caught the soldier a few feet from his rifle, which would be the final deciding factor in this fight. The two rolled in the sand, trading punches and kicks, biting, scratching, seeking any weapon to gain an advantage.

"Hold it, you two!" The unmistakable accent of a Cockney docker. The two antagonists looked up in the faint light of the moon and saw the man pointing a sten-gun in their general direction.

"Thank God you're 'ere". James could not believe his ears. The German had addressed the docker in a cockney accent.

"You've come to pick me up" James said, hastily. "This man is a German soldier. Kill him"

"Hey, I'm a British officer disguised for a special operation", retorted the German. James could see the indecision in the docker's eyes, an indecision which would cost both of them their lives if he made a wrong choice. Addressing the German, James asked "Where's the trouble and strife?"

The German's eyes narrowed, imperceptibly. His mind went back to the language lessons he had endured in the early days of the war. He knew there was trickery in such a banal question, but where was it? And then it occurred to him. The biggest risk, often discussed in the lessons, was the letter 'w', pronounced by Germans as the English pronounce 'v'. With studied concentration the soldier replied, with perfect English pronunciation.

"In wartime, there is trouble and strife all over the world". With this he knew he had pronounced the 'w' in the English fashion, won enough *time, sown enough doubt in the mind of the docker. In a moment he would spring into action and bring an end to this affair. The docker's eyes fixed on the German, who had not known that 'trouble and strife' was Cockney rhyming slang for 'wife', an omission entirely unusual for the normally thorough Wehrmacht educational department.*

The German's answer had been nonsense, and certainly not one that would have been given by any genuine Cockney. Yet still the docker was reluctant to pull the trigger, killing someone who seemed just like himself. An unexpected development then brought matters to a head. In the distance was the sound, growing louder, of a motorbike. James said, "That will be the Gestapo. They'll be here in a few minutes. I am Lieutenant James Courtney. You have come to pick me up. This is an enemy soldier. Kill him". Still the docker hesitated, but then the German, losing his nerve, made a fatal mistake. He leapt to where his rifle lay. Before he could lift the weapon, he was cut in half by a blast from the docker's sten-gun. "Let's move, quick."

James raced to where he had left Henri's unconscious body, and with his last reserves of strength, hauled him onto his shoulders. Staggering under the weight, he reached the boat just as the motorbike came to a halt. He reckoned it would take two minutes to get beyond the range of the machine guns the SS troops would certainly carry. This was going to be close! The docker gunned the engine into life. With a roar the boat surged into the darkness. In a few minutes, now beyond range, and grateful that the Germans had been unable to focus adequately, James looked up over the stern of the boat. The beach was lit up by the headlights of the motorbike and the accompanying troop carrier. They were wasting ammunition, pouring it into the sea in a futile attempt to assuage their commander's rage. As he gazed at the receding shoreline, James looked straight into the eyes of Sturmbannfuehrer Otto Stockhausen, of the Geheimstaatspolizei, the infamous and ubiquitous Gestapo, who glared back, as if only inches away, with an insane, enraged, hatred.

Chapter 2

Aldershot barracks. Midday 7th June

"The report states that you suffered lacerations, minor burns, severe bruising and grazing. Henri's the same, but with a broken leg. Quite a complication. He will be in plaster for two months". Colonel Sir Charles

Crayne, a senior officer of Special Operations Executive, looked James directly in the eye.

"Is there anything you wish to add to this report?"

"Sir, I wish it to be known that the master of the vessel sent to pick me up acted above and beyond the call of duty. He remained at the scene long after the rendezvous hour and he intervened when the outcome was not at all clear. It is not an exaggeration to say that he probably saved my life".

"Obviously, I'm very grateful for that...", Sir Charles interrupted. "I assume you mean the fracas with the German sentry. I've made the point several times to the Chiefs of Combined Ops and the answer is always the same. 'We haven't got the resources to train naval personnel for tasks like this, so agents on clandestine missions must rely on their own capabilities'. Thanks for nothing". James nodded in agreement, but both men knew that resources were seriously stretched, especially now that the invasion of the European mainland was underway.

"James, I need to put you fully in the picture. You are aware that yesterday was D-Day. Well, according to our intelligence, the Germans are NOT aware of that. They think it's a diversionary attack to draw their powerful 15th Army away from its positions around Calais, where they expect the real invasion. The reason they think this is because of the success of Operation Fortitude, the operation you've been involved in for the last year. It is an operation, still underway, to deceive the enemy about the real landing sites. So, far from being the costly failure you think your last mission was, the mere fact that the attack on the listening post at Foin was attempted at all indicates to the Germans that we are trying to soften up the defenses in the area around Calais. The longer they believe this, the better chance our lads have of securing the beaches. Even now, with Allied troops and materials pouring into Normandy, the 15th Army hasn't moved" Sir Charles looked at James. He knew exactly what was in the younger man's mind. "James, I want you to know that my orders were to use the best men we had for Fortitude. We've lost men, good men, on what may seem to you a sideshow, but believe me....." It was James' turn to interrupt.

"Sir, I fully understand the importance of the operation. I can see that it is vital that the Germans are convinced to keep their main defenses in Calais. In your position, I would have done the same".

Sir Charles was silently grateful for these words from a man he held in such high regard. After a few moments Sir Charles said. "James, you have a couple of weeks leave. Where will you be taking it?"

"Well, Sir, I was thinking that I might make a short trip to visit a young lady of our mutual acquaintance over at Bishops' Lodge, unless you can think of a better idea".

"No I can't, my boy. She's been constantly probing since you went back on 'Coastal command'. Unfortunately, with all that's going on I won't be able to get over until the weekend at the earliest. By then the situation in France will be a little clearer and I will be able to let you know what is really going on"

"I'll look forward to that. In the mean-time I'd better get a move on or else I'll be in serious trouble. I've been back almost 10 hours and not yet got in touch".

With that the men shook hands warmly and saluted each other. James departed for the short trip to Bishops' Lodge the home of Sir Charles Crayne and his daughter Charlotte, the only woman James had ever loved. As he watched James leave the building Sir Charles thought again of the tragic circumstances that had brought James into his life. James' father had been a highly successful banker, a career interrupted for the duration by the First World War. Married in 1915, he had been blessed in 1919 with a son, James, and a year later, with a second son, Simon. The family had lost everything in the 1929 financial crash and, unable to face an uncertain future, Courtney senior had taken his own life. Two years later James' mother, grief stricken and heart broken, was dead. James, now thirteen years old, had been taken in by a friend of his father, who happened also to be an acquaintance of Sir Charles. Simon had been taken in by an aunt in London.

Sir Charles had served in the Great War, entering as a second lieutenant from military college in 1914. By 1915 he had been promoted to Major and had finally come through the maelstrom physically unhurt. He shared the silent mental anguish of his experiences with all the others who had survived. He chose to stay in the army after the end of hostilities, thereby maintaining the family tradition of military service. Bishops' Lodge was a substantial estate where his family had lived for three generations after his great-grandfather had secured ownership by dubious means which the family never discussed. The main residential building, where he and Charlotte now lived, was adequate without being over-sized. There were several other apartments which were capable of housing other branches of the family in reasonable privacy, but they preferred to live mainly in London. A number of tenant farmers ran the farm on behalf of the family, and this provided a sufficient and secure income.

In 1920 Sir Charles married the daughter of a general officer. The relationship had been happy, and, a year later, Charlotte had been born. A year further on a son had been stillborn. After this, no further pregnancy could be contemplated due to his wife's condition. In 1931, James had become the son Sir Charles had craved. His wife was happy at the arrival in their lives of this healthy young man, and Sir Charles noted with satisfaction the growing relationship between his own daughter and the orphan living with the family of his friend and neighbor. He was particularly pleased that it seemed James would pursue a military career.

At school James had shown little interest in studies, but had, nevertheless, won a place at Oxford University. Here he continued to devote the minimum amount of time to study, preferring instead to concentrate on sports and social matters. Such was his natural aptitude that by the time he left Oxford he had secured a military commission and was fluent in French and German.

Thinking it best to advise her of his imminent arrival, James had stopped to make a phone-call to Charlotte. He inserted the coins and listened as the system dragged itself into action. On hearing her pick up the phone and announce the number he breathed deliberately and heavily.

"James". Her voice was filled with excitement as he performed this familiar routine.

"CC darling! How come you are never afraid when I make dirty phone calls?"

"I'm used to it. It happens every-day. It's the most exciting part of the day. What else has a lonely woman to look forward to?"

"You won't be lonely much longer. I've got two weeks leave".

"Where are you? When will you be here?" Her voice was filled with a delicious anticipation.

"Well actually, I'm at the station, with a taxi waiting and I'll be with you in fifteen minutes"

"I'll be ready". There was a tinge of seduction to her voice.

"In that case, I'll be ten"

A frisson of excitement raced through her body as she replaced the receiver. In ten minutes he'd be there, with two whole weeks together. She rushed upstairs to shower and change; by the time she had finished, the taxi was at the door. She reached the bottom of the stairs as the doorbell rang. She slid back the bolt and threw herself into James' outstretched arms. They embraced and kissed as if they had been apart for months. In fact, it was just over a week. After a few endless moments he picked up his case and she led him into the lounge. They sat down on the settee and he kissed her again, not, this time, the kiss of people reunited, but the kiss of lovers, deeper, gently, and with a subdued but growing passion. He looked deeply into her eyes; stroked her hair and face. "Your father can't get here until later tomorrow". His words said less than his eyes.

"What a pity". Her voice was tinged with the seductive irony of a woman completely secure, entirely in tune with the man she loved. He left his case in the lounge and followed her upstairs, where they made love until the late evening.

"What do you want to do now?". Charlotte's voice was relaxed.
"Rest and recuperate" She laughed girlishly at his feigned exhaustion.
"We can eat here or at the 'Old Inn'
"Let's not venture out tonight. Let's listen to the wireless for a while"
She left him in the lounge and went to the kitchen to prepare a late meal. There was no-one else in the house, so they could dine in their preferred informal manner. She quickly produced a hearty buffet with strong English cider. When she returned to the lounge, James was listening intently to the radio. There was a further bulletin about the Normandy landings. In the unexcited, deadpan manner of British military announcements the newscaster was informing the British public that on D-Day 156000 Allied troops had reached France with all their equipment intact. She whooped with joy at the thought that the war would soon be over, but James was much more somber, knowing the enormous problems which lay ahead for the Allies.

"I assume you were on 'Coastal' duties last week?" She tried to sound merely conversational, but James knew that this was the beginning of a gentle interrogation about his activities. The story of coastal duties had been concocted by James and Sir Charles as a means of concealing from Charlotte the true, hazardous, nature of James' secret missions.

"Yes. I had to stand in for a fellow who was taken ill. We patrolled the area around Dover to.."

"..watch out for enemy saboteurs." She completed the sentence she had heard so many times. "And why is it necessary to have an army officer on board?"

"Darling, I've told you before. An army officer is best able to assess the significance of an enemy landing".

Charlotte had heard that before, as well. She decided to try a different line.

"Was there anything worth reporting. Any incursions, any attempted enemy landings, any danger of any sort?" His mind flashed back to the near disastrous mission to Foin, and his encounter with the sentry.

"Yes, in the early morning gloom one of the lookouts, normally a very sound chap, thought he saw a U-Boat. There was quite a panic for a couple of hours, but nothing further was revealed, so either there was no submarine, or it beat a hasty retreat".

"What about the bruises on your body?"

"You always get those when you are at sea in choppy conditions. You don't even notice at the time, and then later on you wonder where they came from". A neat explanation, he thought. Covered everything. She would not believe it, of course, but this way she could be spared the anguish she would otherwise have to endure if she knew the true nature of the risks he ran as a matter of routine.

After this, their conversation ranged over the wider subject of the invasion. He was warmed to hear of her great admiration of the men who went in first, and those on covert missions, the airborne and paratroop forces whose job it was to degrade the defenses to ease the way, as far as possible, for the invasion proper. They speculated over the likely duration of the War now that the Allies were back on the mainland of Europe. He admitted that Coastal Command would become less important and that he would probably be re-deployed, but he didn't know what he would be doing. All would be revealed when Sir Charles arrived on Saturday evening.

It had been a long and tiring day. Shortly before midnight she went upstairs to her bedroom and quickly fell into a deep sleep. James read the newspapers for a while and then made his way to the spare bedroom.

Chapter 4

Bishops' Lodge 07.00 hours 10th June

Cook was the first member of Sir Charles' staff to arrive. She had her own key to the staff entrance and had been the unofficial housekeeper since the death of lady Crayne in 1941. She immediately began to prepare breakfast for Charlotte, unaware as yet of James' presence. As usual, Charlotte arose at 7.30 and showered. After this she went directly to the kitchen with the news that there would be a guest for two weeks, so that cook could make appropriate changes to her plans. She then took a pot of tea to the guest room where James was, seemingly, still in a deep sleep. She watched him for a few moments and then kissed him gently.

"If I had been a spy, you'd be a goner by now".

James smiled. "You were in my sights the moment you entered the room".

She kissed him again and then asked, "What would you like to do today?" James thought for a few moments. His special role meant that he could be called on to return for a mission if an emergency arose, even when he was officially on leave. It had been four days since he had done any substantial exercise, and it would be another two before he could do even rudimentary fitness training. For someone in his position, whose very life may depend on his level of fitness, this was too long a period of inactivity. "I think if we do a couple of gentle hours of tennis this morning and then take a walk down to the village after lunch we will have earned a few hours in the Old Inn".

At 09.30 they set off for the tennis courts. It was a warm day with a clear blue sky. They spoke little as they drove to the club, each being immersed in their own thoughts. James, having read the morning paper, was trying to imagine the situation in the invasion area. Charlotte was trying to unravel the mystery of the man sitting next to her. She knew that James was an accomplished sportsman, but also that he was, for some inexplicable reason, hopeless at tennis. In this one sport his co-ordination was below par, his timing sadly deficient. In the early days of their relationship she had thought he was allowing her to win. She had always won, every single game they had played. Even though she was a good tennis player this seemed strange to her. Gradually, it had dawned on her that he just could not master tennis. This fact did not prevent him from putting enormous effort into each game, but always it ended in frustration. Occasionally, she had deliberately allowed him to win a few points, but it had become obvious to him and he had asked her not to do this. His frustration would dissipate rapidly, and it had never caused any problems in their relationship. So, she would play her normal game, with her maximum, considerable ability, and win effortlessly. From his point of view, it was the exercise that mattered.

There was no-one at the tennis club except the solitary grounds-man. After the usual pleasantries and payment of the fee, they changed and began to play.Charlotte dominated the game, with James struggling to put up any decent kind of opposition. She admired his determination to try to return every ball, even those impossibly beyond his reach. As the morning grew warmer she was amazed to see how James could maintain the torrid pace he always set for himself. By now his kit was soaked with sweat and still there was no let-up. Finally, she delivered a superb shot which left James wrong footed and well out of position.

Nevertheless, he raced across the court to try to retrieve the shot, but narrowly missed connecting with the ball.

She then saw a sight which she had seen many times before, and which had caused her concern in the initial stages of their friendship. James stood upright, his head held up as if looking at the sky, his left hand at his throat and his right hand on his hip. He stood completely still in this position for several moments. Charlotte knew that this was his way of dispelling his anger and frustration; she had seen this many times, and now accepted it as a normal mannerism. Sure enough, after a few moments, he turned to her and shot her a genuinely affectionate smile.

"OK, you win this time. Let's call it a day. As you are so good at tennis, I will take you to visit Paris as soon as conditions allow." This was a reference to the situation a few years earlier when, as a girl at school, Charlotte had been involved in a student exchange with a school in Paris. At the last minute, the family she would be staying with in Paris had to withdraw. She was heartbroken by the disappointment, and inconsolable, until James had promised, one day, to take her there. The fulfilment of this promise was delayed by the outbreak of war, but it remained a dream for both of them. She smiled back at him, grateful that he was able to cope so well with the situation.

It had been a good session for the main purpose. James felt that he could now relax for the remainder of the weekend. He was looking forward to the rest of the day alone with Charlotte, and also the arrival, later that day, of Sir Charles, when he would discover what his Commanding Officer had in store for him.

Chapter 5

19.00hours 10th June 1944 Bishop's Lodge

"Of course, it's all a matter of opinion, and I can assure you that opinion is very divided.

Monty, needless to say, wants to monopolize all the supplies for a major offensive across Northern Germany in order to finish the war this year, whilst the American commanders, between you and me, are not too keen on a Brit getting all the glory, whatever the merits or otherwise of Monty's plans. In any case it's all academic at the moment because there is much to be achieved before any such ambitious campaign can be contemplated. There is at least one thing that everyone agrees on; the Germans cannot now win the war, and it's only a question of who gets to Berlin first, the Russians or us, and how we can minimize the loss of life in the meantime. Then, we've got to decide how to govern Germany and what to do with the present Government, who, I suspect, will be tried for war crimes". As Sir Charles spoke these last words Charlotte entered the room, where Sir Charles and James had spent the whole evening discussing the latest developments.

"Quite right too," she said, as she kissed her father and James. "Some of the officers' wives were talking this afternoon, and do you know what the Nazis have done? Murder. Plain, simple murder. They've killed innocent civilians, men, women and children, mainly Jewish people. And do you have any idea how many? Perhaps as many as sixty thousand. Sixty thousand! Sixty thousand innocent people, non-combatants, defenseless people".

James and Sir Charles looked blankly at each other. "It may be that we only know half the story". Sir Charles' reply was meek, non-committal. There was no need to make public their suspicions as to the full horror at this stage.

"I only hope you are wrong!" The telephone had started ringing, so that these were Charlotte's last words on the subject. She left the room to deal with the phone call.

"James, let me continue what we were talking about before she got back. As I was saying, it is remotely possible that the war will end this year, or, more likely, around summer of next. But there is one thing that is worrying the planners. The Austrian Alps is a formidable range of mountains, largely impassable in winter, and would be a difficult nut to crack if it were fortified. And this is just what they think might happen. As the war turns more and more against Germany, it is considered possible that the Nazis will built a National Redoubt and conduct a last-ditch guerrilla campaign from there. Personally, I don't believe this is a viable option, but they will be desperate men, facing defeat, who care little for Germany and her people, and if they did decide to take that course of action, the cost of clearing them out would be very high in terms of time and lives lost. Now, we have agents in the region who will keep us informed of any increase in activity, so we can make a judgement about what is going on. If we believe that arms and munitions are being moved in and that the threat is real, we will need a tough, well trained, mobile force, skilled in alpine warfare to occupy the area and disrupt the Nazis' plans. It has been agreed that we will provide a force of two thousand men, and the Americans four thousand. We expect that it won't be needed until, say, February, but I want you to get on with training as soon as possible, because some of them will be inexperienced in combat. What do you think?"

"Where will the training take place?" asked James.

"There is a disused Air Force base at Holmbury, in Kent, where the initial training, your stuff, will take place, and then they will be moved to Scotland for further training. You will be based exclusively at Holmbury and concentrating on fitness, small arms matters and unarmed combat".

"And when do you want me to start?"

"Thank you, James. You will have four hundred men, and training is due to start on Thursday, 22nd June, but, given the current circumstances, I would not expect full turnout until the following Monday. Things are likely to be a bit chaotic at first, so, no change there. One other thing; we've always had to be available to deal with emergencies in our line of operations, as you know better than most, and this Corps is no different in that respect. You may be called upon at short notice."

Charlotte entered the room. "That was Simon. He'd heard you were on leave, and he's coming over for a few days next week. He'll be here on Tuesday, at around midday. Now, tell me. What is the big secret? What are your new duties?"

"I have asked James to undertake training duties for the next few months, and he'll be stationed in Kent, so you will be able to see each other a bit more often".

"Oh good. How amazing the military are? It is remarkable that three years on Coastal Command qualifies you to train soldiers". Her tone was heavily ironic.

"You are far too inquisitive, young lady. It's only low-key stuff, drill and that sort of thing. Time to open a bottle, I think." This was Sir Charles' way of bringing a discussion to an end, and Charlotte knew that there was nothing to be gained by further enquiry.

Chapter 6

13.00 hours 12th June SS Headquarters Calais

The soldier sat uneasily. He had no idea why he had been plucked from the Russian front and brought 1000 miles to attend the funeral of his brother. It was unheard of for someone of his lowly rank to be afforded this privilege. Still, he wasn't complaining. Anything was preferable to the constant danger and discomfort of the Eastern Front. The silence was broken by the brittle voice on the orderly's intercom, ordering that the soldier be shown in to the Commanders' office. He was struck by the sheer size and grandeur of the office. Made of oak panels and lined with bookshelves it resembled the study of an academic rather than a military establishment. Behind the large, imposing desk sat the new Commander for the Calais district, Obergruppenfuehrer

Stockhausen. The soldier stood rigidly to attention. After a few moments, Stockhausen looked up and gazed at the soldier. "Sit down, Korporal Schumm" Despite his feelings of awkwardness, he sat where the officer had indicated.

"You have been brought here on my express orders to attend the funeral of your brother. I feel I owe him this in view of the exemplary service he has provided for me and for the Fatherland. I want you to know that your brother was one of our most admired and respected soldiers. Brave, resourceful and much loved by his comrades. If we had more like him, the Allies would even now be licking their wounds, instead of unloading men and materials in Northern France. I can assure you that if he had not been murdered by a British officer, your brother was destined for great things after the war".

Schumm was confused. The notification he had received merely stated 'killed in action'. To hear this now was a complete surprise. Stockhausen continued. "I see from your files that you have lost three brothers in the struggle, and that you are the last of the males of your family. Please allow me to say, on behalf of the Fuehrer, that we all feel and share your pain. However, I must point out that we are at war, and none of us can allow our personal feelings to take precedence over the needs of the Fatherland even, as in this case, where circumstances are exceptional, and where retribution is possible. The funeral is tomorrow, at 09.00 hours sharp. Afterwards, you will be allowed one days' rest and then you will be returned to your unit. Dismissed". Stockhausen had used every psychological trick he knew, and now he could only wait for the desired reaction.

Dazed, korporal Schumm stood up and saluted smartly. He turned to leave the room, but hesitated. "Sir. You said that my brother had been murdered. I was only informed that he had been killed in action."

Stockhausen looked deeply into the soldier's eyes for a long moment. He said, mildly, "Sit down". Schumm resumed his seat. "Your brother had been stationed at a small barracks near St. Michel. It's a quiet area where we send men who have performed well for a short break from the routines of army life. If anyone deserved a break, it was your brother. On the night he died, we were, as usual, under heavy air attack. He had been posted as sentry for that night, so he was patrolling outside the barracks when a stray bomb exploded on the building, causing considerable damage. True to form your brother plunged into the inferno and rescued three of his comrades. But, unknown to him, a British agent had been active in the area, and he and five resistance men attacked the burning barracks. One of the men your brother rescued survived, and his story is that your brother put up a heroic struggle, killing three of his adversaries, but finally, sheer weight of numbers overwhelmed him. His hands and feet were bound behind his back and he was laid face down on the ground". Stockhausen paused to exaggerate the drama of his next sentence. "Then the British agent took out a knife and slit your brother's throat".

With an anguished cry Schumm leapt from his chair. It was just the reaction Stockhausen had hoped for. "Bring some brandy". The order was barked into the intercom. Moments later the orderly entered the room. The soldier threw back the warming spirit, and then a second, and a third. Stunned and tormented, he resumed his seat. Stockhausen dismissed the orderly. He lowered his eyes and said nothing, leaving the soldier with his thoughts.

After a few minutes Schumm said, "Sir, you said that we had the means to take revenge on this murderer. I feel, Sir, that I should have the right to avenge my brother".

"Don't you think I want to do the same? Don't you think I feel the same anger and outrage that you do? Your brother was like a son to me"

"Then you must help me, Sir. For both our sakes". There was pleading in Schumm's eyes.   This was better than Stockhausen had hoped. For a moment he held the soldier's eyes with his own, and then slumped back into his chair. "Sit down, Schumm". He allowed a few minutes to elapse in silence. "Right. I will order my staff to prepare a plan. But be aware, it will be dangerous, and it will mean a visit to England. If you are captured, you will be shot as a spy".

"If there is a chance to remove this scum from the face of the earth, it will be worth it, Sir. I will not fail"

Stockhausen arranged for suitable accommodation to be provided for the soldier, whom he ordered to return in two days for further instructions. After Schumm had gone to his billet, Stockhausen sat back in his chair. A malevolent smile spread across his face as he considered his plans for Lieutenant Courtney, codenamed 'Hotel'. He had realized that the game was up for the Nazis soon after the military disasters in North Africa and Stalingrad. For all the Fuehrer's talk about 'miracle weapons' and 'fighting to the last man' it was clear that the Allies had vastly superior resources and manpower, and, in Stalin at least, a leader who was, like Hitler, prepared to pay any price in terms of human life sacrificed. He was glad that he had started to salt away plenty of stolen wealth to guard against the possibility that he might have to leave Europe fairly quickly.

Now, with substantial assets hidden in Canada, Mexico and Switzerland, and with Allied forces pouring into Northern France, as well as millions of Russians attacking from the East, it was time to start making detailed arrangements for his escape. All that was needed before this was to settle scores with those who were his personal enemies; and there was no man whom Stockhausen hated more than James Courtney, an agent of the British Special Operations Executive, codename; Hotel.

Chapter 7

13.00 hours 13th June Bramall Moor Railway station

It was one of those long, warm, peaceful afternoons that older people associate with their younger days. James and Charlotte were sitting on a wooden bench outside the railway station. Sir Charles had returned to his Headquarters, having given James the final instruction that he should go to Holmbury in good time to arrange his personal accommodation before the arrival of the men in his charge.

The train arrived a few minutes late, shortly after one o'clock. Simon descended from one of the center compartments, carrying his mid-blue Royal Air Force (R.A.F) grip. He had been a Spitfire pilot during the Battle of Britain, one of those immortalized by Churchill's description as 'the few'. For two or three months during the Summer of 1940, 'the few' had been in the vanguard of Britain's defense against the overwhelming numerical superiority of the German 'Luftwaffe', Hitler's hitherto invincible Air Force. In those desperate times they had often been scrambled at the last moment to intercept German attacks. During this period Simon had flown sortie after sortie, often without respite in the hours of daylight. It had been a close-run fight for mere survival, the Royal Air Force being regarded as the only military unit capable of inflicting unacceptable damage on an invading force. The loss rate suffered by the R.A.F. had been alarming, but the kill-rate against the enemy had been devastating. Such had been the numerical superiority enjoyed by Germany that R.A.F. Fighter command had been on the verge of collapse in late August when, in a crucial error, the Germans turned their attention to attacking civilian targets. This enabled the R.A.F. to reorganize, and, within a few days, such were the losses suffered by the Germans that they postponed Operation Sealion, the plan to invade Britain. For the remaining months of 1940, and all of '41 and '42 Simon had been involved in training younger pilots. In 1943 he joined R.A.F. intelligence. Simon's fiancee, also involved in intelligence, was unable to take leave at the same time as Simon to visit Bishops Lodge. As they lived near to each other, and worked closely, Simon thought a few days apart would not be too much of a hardship.

After the brothers exchanged a warm greeting it was agreed that, as Henri was due on the next train, following his medical treatment for injuries suffered whilst with James in the latest foray against the Germans in Northern France, it was sensible to wait at the local pub, just half a mile from the station. It was one of those old-established, oak-beamed hostelries much admired by seekers of Olde England. They decided to occupy one of the tables outside, and James went to the bar. He emerged shortly with a tray of beer and sandwiches. It was apparent that Charlotte had asked Simon about his duties.

"...mainly to do with photographic reconnaissance. You'd be surprised how difficult it can be at first to identify people and objects when viewed from above. On the other hand, after a few months practice you can assess photos fairly well, even when camouflage is used. So, we can inform ground forces of the strength of opposition they are likely to face over any given route, and this helps them to decide the best way forward. It's an important job, because if we get it wrong and a lightly armed force is sent against a heavily fortified enemy position, this could result in the waste of many lives".

"Yes, I can see that". Charlotte was glad that she didn't have to make such assessments.

"And how goes the War from the point of view of R.A.F. intelligence?" James had learned from his own experience the value of information supplied by Simon's people.

"We're reasonably satisfied with our performance in 99% of what we do."

"Yes, but it's the results of the other 1% that matters, isn't it?" Charlotte's interruption caused Simon to smile.

"It ALL matters", he replied politely, but some of it is impossible to assess. For example, for weeks we've been receiving photos of an area near Calais where the Germans are building some installations. So, we know something is going on. Often, you can tell from its size and location what it is going to be, and often, just as important, what it's NOT going to be. This particular site is not like a typical barracks, and not situated within range of any significant strategic objective. So, it is part of the 1% of, as yet, unsatisfactory intelligence. By the way, James, I have a self-loading, semi-automatic pistol for you, direct from a German pilot, as you requested."

"I presume it's a Luger?"

"It's a Luger Parabellum. Almost unused. The magazine full, and a spare magazine as well."

"Can someone tell me what you are talking about". Charlotte was genuinely in the dark on this subject. James started to explain.

"Fighter pilots are routinely armed with a pistol, a personal weapon for use if they are shot down, and are lucky enough to survive..." Simon interrupted. "The purpose of this personal weapon has been a matter of some disagreement. Some believe it is to be used for self-defense. The problem with this is that, if you land in enemy territory and are captured by ordinary citizens, it is likely that you would be lynched, after a fairly brutal beating. You have, after all, just been trying to destroy their homes and lives. So, it might be better to use, shall we say, just one bullet...this would at least save you from the vengeance of the mob. On the other hand, if you were captured by military personnel, you would expect to be treated with some respect, as you may have valuable information. In that case, shooting at your captors would seem a fairly pointless exercise. Needless to say, German pilots have similar personal weapons, and these are highly prized trophies, especially Luger pistols"

"So, why don't you want to keep it for yourself". Charlotte asked.

"I have been very lucky in the last few years. I have survived being shot down over Kent and have had the privilege of capturing a Luftwaffe pilot, shot down in the same engagement. He was happy to surrender to me rather than take his chances with the mob. Naturally, I confiscated his personal weapon. This..." Simon regarded his fingernails, breathed on them and rubbed then against his tunic "has happened twice. Hence, one gift for the, ahem.......less heroic brother."

"Point taken", replied Charlotte.

"It's time, Mr. James, sir". The landlord called from within to indicate, as James had requested, that the next train was due. They quickly finished their drinks and set off for the station.

Henri had been discharged from hospital the previous day and arrived with his leg in plaster. He walked awkwardly, with the aid of crutches. He and James had met through an exchange holiday during their schooldays, and had remained friends since then, communicating regularly and visiting each-others' home once a year, until the outbreak of war disrupted these arrangements. Charlotte had known Henri for almost as long as James. A wave of panic suddenly hit James. Inevitably Charlotte would ask him about his broken leg, and James had not thought to agree a story with Henri which would keep Charlotte in the dark about the nature of James' activities.

"Henri, my friend. It's months since I've seen you. How are you? What have you done to your leg?" James had quickly taken the initiative and put Henri on his guard. For his part, Henri was taken aback by these comments, but did not show it. Clearly, the truth was not required.

"I'm ashamed to tell you, mon ami. Simon, how are you? And Charlotte, beautiful as ever. I would have contacted you sooner, but I have been secretly in England for three weeks. I was due to go into

Normandy in a spearhead operation in the first few hours of the invasion to assist with the locals. Believe it or not, I broke my leg in the last hour before embarkation when I tripped n I'm afraid". His eyes met James', and they smiled at the fiction. By the time they reached Bishop's Lodge the discussion of Henri's injury had reached the point where the invasion had almost been postponed because of it. James intended to continue this banter until he could put Simon and Henri in the picture about the situation. An opportunity soon arose when Charlotte announced her intention to make a few phone calls. When she returned they were discussing James' new duties. As well as explaining his preference for keeping Charlotte in the dark about the dangerous situations he had been in, he had given Simon and Henri full details of the purpose of his new commission.

"The training will involve unarmed combat, weapons, and camouflage techniques. Oh, and the use of some French and German language".

"What would be the point of that?" Charlotte was genuinely puzzled.

"As commandos they can be called upon at any time to carry out unusual duties, sometimes behind enemy lines." replied James. "If you were confronted by a German soldier, it could give you valuable seconds as well as the element of surprise if you were able to say a few things in French, or even better, in German. Perhaps, Henri, as you're laid up for a couple of months you would like to join me and help out with the French?"

"I have no other plans, mon ami"
That situation dealt with, they made plans for the remainder of their leave.

Chapter 8

19.00 hours 16th June SS HQ Calais

Everything that could be anticipated had been attended to. All that was required now was that Schumm was still willing to go, still prepared to take the chance. Stockhausen had chosen one of his most trusted men to keep the corporal angry, to talk to him about the 'murder' of his hero brother. The interview that would take place in the next few minutes would decide whether Stockhausen would be able to achieve his desired revenge on Hotel. Schumm had arrived early for his orders, a good sign.

"Sit down, korporal". Stockhausen hoped he sounded professional, matter of fact, and not betraying too much anxiety. "My staff were rather surprised that I had decided to put at your disposal the resources that I have made available. Some of them think of you as an outsider, an unknown quantity. But, I think I am a good judge of men, and I believe that you are the man for the job. We have put together a bold plan for the abduction and bringing to justice of the Englishman who murdered your brother. For success, the plan requires you to impersonate an English soldier. As you are fluent in English and have a military bearing this will not be a problem, especially as we will provide you with genuine British documents and equipment. I have an agent who has provided all the information we need for this operation". Stockhausen passed across his desk a large, bulky envelope. "This contains your documents and a detailed outline of your orders. Briefly, the plan is as follows. You will be landed on the English coast at 22.00 hours on Wednesday, 21st June. You will make your way to Holmbury Air Force base, where your target, lieutenant James Courtney is due to start training more of his own kind over the next few days. My agent assures me that there will be no other personnel on the base until the following week. You will introduce yourself and be assigned a barracks. There will be some confusion, with you arriving alone, but there is always confusion when new units are set up. You and he will be alone for the next several hours. You must use this time to win his confidence and then overpower him. Do NOT underestimate him. He is a vicious killer. We prefer him alive, but if you have to kill him there and then, so be it. Above all, we want YOU back here safely. If you have to kill him, bring his body back here. A French transport plane will land on Thursday night at about 23.00 hours, so make sure that the landing lights are switched on at 22.30. The flight time from Holmbury to Calais is about one hour, and I shall be waiting to take charge of the prisoner when you return. Do you have any questions?"

"No, Sir."

"I understand your desire for immediate revenge, but this man can give us much information. Killing him is the worst outcome, short of not capturing him at all. Remember, you have all the advantages. You should be able to carry out your orders exactly. Whatever happens, bring yourself back safely. Men like you are hard to replace" This was clearly the end of the interview.

"I will not fail, Sir. Heil Hitler".

Stockhausen saluted the corporal who was then escorted from the office and taken back to his billet to study his orders. He was excited at the chance to avenge his brother and to be perhaps the only German soldier to invade the British mainland.

Stockhausen unlocked a drawer in his desk and extracted two files. One was marked 'Hotel' and contained detailed information about James

Courtney, plus background information on Sir Charles, Charlotte and Simon. He skipped through the pages, which he knew almost by heart, pausing only to gaze at a photograph of James. After a few moments he returned the papers to the folder and gave his attention to the second file, entitled 'British Imperial Colonies'. In seven days Hotel would be his guest, and in nine days, that file could be closed forever. In the meantime, he would have to decide where he would live after the defeat of Germany. With his several genuine passports from several occupied countries there would be no difficulty in emigrating, especially with his forged academic qualifications. His secret wealth would provide a comfortable retirement. He had narrowed the choice down to Canada or Australia. He must decide soon which it was to be.

Chapter 9
Midday 21st June Bishop's Lodge

It had been fifteen days since the invasion of Europe by the Allies. In his head James knew that he had done his share, and more, in the battle against Germany's fascist leaders, and yet he felt that his two weeks of leave were, somehow, a betrayal of all the other men in uniform. He had expressed these sentiments to Sir Charles and to Henri, who had both mocked the idea that James was not doing enough. Now, it was time for him to go to Holmbury in preparation for his new role as Commanding Officer.

Enthusiastic as he was to begin this period of his wartime contribution, he was also sad at the thought of leaving Charlotte, with whom he had spent a blissful fortnight.

"You'll be twenty-seven miles away, and I'll see you every Saturday", had been her reply to his comments on the matter. He knew Charlotte well enough to know that, however emotional she could be at times, she was, in fact, incorrigibly practical.

"All right. Henri and I will tootle over to Holmbury and start setting things up, and we'll be back in time for lunch on Saturday". At that moment Henri entered the room. "OK, Henri? Best foot forward", a comment not designed to help his French ally through the increasingly frustrating period of semi-immobility. "Only another month until the cast comes off". Five minutes later they had left Bishop's Lodge in Charlotte's car, which they had borrowed for a few days, and were on their way to Holmbury.

James had been told that it was a disused Air Force base, and this had conjured up an image of semi derelict buildings and a runway overgrown with weeds. In fact, it had been converted for Army use several months earlier. It had been used to house troops earmarked for day one of the invasion. He was pleasantly surprised to find that the massive hangars had been refurbished into proper barracks, and that the CO's office, which was adjacent to the main office, was furnished to a reasonable degree of luxury, a fact which made up for it's too close proximity to the runway. He wondered if the previous occupant had been an American. A brief inspection showed that all the facilities were in proper working order.

When they arrived, James and Henri found the base deserted. It was unusual for a senior officer to arrive in such circumstances, but Sir Charles had warned James that so much effort was being put into the Normandy offensive that all resources were in short supply, so he would have to make do as best he could. James offered to share the CO's accommodation with Henri. It had been a polite gesture, but one which Henri refused. He would take a bunk in the smaller barracks just adjacent to the office, only a few yards away. Having unloaded their luggage, James put a call through to Charlotte. He gave her a brief description of the base, and they exchanged a few words of affection. As an afterthought, he gave her the phone number of the base. As he replaced the receiver there was a knock at the door.

"Come in". The door opened. A tall, well made soldier entered.

"Private John Lens, Sir. Transferred from Wessex Fusiliers to 420 Commando. I'm not actually due here until Monday, Sir, but there was transport coming this way, so I took the chance of getting that".

"Stand easy, private". The soldier offered documents, which James took and examined briefly. This was the most boring, mundane part of the CO's job, dealing with documentation and the thousand and one routine tasks which were necessary in running a military establishment. James hoped that, within a few days, he would be provided with sufficient clerical staff, so that he could get on with his main duties. The papers seemed in order. He handed them back to Lens.   "As you can see we're a bit disorganized at the moment. I expect the non-commissioned officers to arrive tomorrow or Friday. In the meantime, find yourself quarters in the barracks nearest this office. You will find one of the instructors there already". The soldier's heart leapt when he heard this. The presence of an instructor was an unexpected complication. The next few words calmed him. "He's got a broken leg, so help him as much as you can. Carry on"

The soldier saluted smartly and left the office. He made his way to the barracks as instructed, and there he met Henri. Clearly, this was no threat. Henri could be discounted from his plans. The way was clear to carry out his instructions from Stockhausen. He exchanged a few pleasant words of introduction, and then changed into shorts and running shoes. Informing Henri that he intended to do a five-mile run, he left the barracks; better to keep out of the way than have a conversation and risk making a mistake. He ran to the village, a distance he estimated at six kilometers. On his way back, at about 7.00pm he saw approaching him the car which had been parked on the base. He recognized Courtney and the Frenchman. He stopped running and saluted as they passed. He guessed they were on their way to the village for a meal and a few beers. This was so much better than having them on the base, and if they returned the worse for a night's drinking, that would help too. On his arrival back at the base he resisted to temptation to search the COs office. At this early stage there was probably little of value in terms of intelligence, and he would run the risk of leaving something out of place, thereby alerting the Englishman. All he needed now was patience. The waiting was the worst. Each minute seemed to pass so slowly. He felt the heat inside the barracks, oppressive, energy sapping, so he opened two of the windows, unaware of the significance that this would have later. He lay down on his bunk in the dark, until finally, he heard the engine of a car. He climbed into his bed, feigning sleep.

Fifteen minutes later Henri entered the barracks, and softly called a greeting, which the German ignored. It was 9.30. Ideal. Within a quarter of an hour, Henri's breathing was deep and steady. The soldier called Henri's name in a soft voice. No reply, no interruption to the pattern of breathing. He rose from his bunk and noticed from the window that the light in the CO's office was burning. Silently, he crept towards the converted hut where his intended victim was unaware of his approach. A thought occurred to him. Should he knock at the door or just barge in? To knock at this time of night might arouse some suspicion, and he was mindful of Stockhausen's warning not to underestimate his adversary. On the other hand, if he tried to barge in and the door was securely locked, this would be even worse. The problem was resolved when James opened the door to take a final breath of fresh air before retiring.

"Get inside. Do not make any noise" The revolver was pointed directly at James' head. He backed slowly into his office and, on instruction, sat down at his desk. "Good evening, Hotel. You and I are going on a little trip to see a friend of yours. Sturmbannfuehrer Stockhausen awaits your arrival in Calais". James was stunned to hear his codename, which was top secret and known to only a few people. The soldier gave James a pair of shackles and told him to put them on. James played with the idea of resisting but decided against this. It was likely that the soldier, Lens, or whoever he was, would be in a mood to pull the trigger at the first sign of opposition. Better to wait and see what developed.

It was now 22.00 hours. Thirty minutes, before 'Lens' had to turn on the landing lights, and then thirty minutes until the aircraft landed. "Where is the switch for the landing lights?

22.00 hours Bishops Lodge

The force of the 'waves' almost threw Charlotte out of bed. It had been weeks since she had had these feelings. Surely there could be no danger now that James was safely in England. And Henri was with him. And yet the waves pounded her, insistently. Surely there could be no harm in phoning him, even at this hour. She dialed the number of Holmbury base.

22.01 hours Holmbury

James was quite sure that the soldier meant business and decided to play along with him. He might already know where the switch was, so that a lie might antagonize him. "It is in the hangar at the far end of the runway".

"Right. Please accompany me to that place, and do not try any heroics. I am ordered to return you to Calais, dead or alive. Now, move".

The telephone rang. James and the German looked at each other. The ringing seemed oppressively loud. The German considered the options. If the call was ignored, this could be because everyone was asleep, or off base. If the call was answered, a code word for danger could be slipped into the ensuing conversation. "Ignore it". After a few moments, the ringing stopped. "Right, move"

"I need my cap".

"What"?

"It is a matter of common courtesy, and also a condition of the Geneva Convention, that when an officer surrenders, he is allowed to wear full uniform. I need my military cap. It is in my quarters". James gestured towards the door standing ajar, a few feet from where he was seated.   The German eyed James suspiciously. What was there in that room that might be used against him. Should he allow the Englishman to have free rein in this matter. "Wait here. I will get it". He wedged a chair against the door. "If I hear the slightest sound I will be out of that room in one second, and I'll blow your brains out". How stupid this man was, to concern himself with such matters at a time like this, when his life was hanging by a thread. He emerged from the room as few seconds later, with the cap.

James had no idea what the Geneva Convention said about officers who surrendered. 'Surrendered' was a word designed to appeal to the German's vanity, and the cap, a ruse to give him a moment alone in his office. He placed the cap roughly on James' head. All seemed as it had been a few moments ago. But it was not, for James had used those moments to flick the switch, marked 'external', which controlled the telephone. Next time it rang, it would be heard outside courtesy of the outdoor ringer as well as within the office.

Together they moved onto the tarmac. James noticed that the light had been left on in his office and the door was still wide open. The hangar which was their destination was about 1000 yards away, a few minutes' walk, certainly less than five minutes. Now might not be the best time to use his one chance of escape, as the German would be fully alert and nervous. He resisted the temptation to enquire about Henri's fate, as it may not be wise to remind his adversary that there may be another player in this drama, lest he take sensible precautions.

"Do you realize...?" began James.

"Silence. No talking at all". To confirm his intention, he punched James hard on the back of the head. The walk was completed in silence. Above all, thankfully, the phone did not ring.

James wondered who could have called at that hour. Whoever it was, he hoped they would call again in a few minutes. As he approached the hangar he noticed there were no windows on this side, so that the office would not be visible from within. The entrance was on the far side, away from the office. The door, a substantial, reinforced gate, was unlocked. James entered first. As he did so, he felt a blinding pain as his captor smashed the butt of his revolver onto the base of his skull. The German stepped over the unconscious body and fumbled for the light switch. The power was very low, unimproved since the days of the blackouts of 1940. Looking at his watch, the German noted that it would be about thirty minutes before the plane arrived. For all he knew it was even now circling the area. On the wall, beside what appeared to be a large fuse-box, was a lever, with the words LANDING LIGHTS" stenciled above. He pulled the lever and looked outside. It was almost as bright as day, with the runway lit up by brilliant white, green and red lights. There was nothing to do now but wait and listen for the sound of aircraft engines.

Chapter 10

22.18 hours Bishops' Lodge

Charlotte wondered why the 'waves' had lifted so suddenly. Perhaps there had been some small, alarming event, which had now passed. But, passed it had. She now felt completely calm. There was no need to worry. There was nothing to be done. She got back into bed. In a few moments, she believed, she would be blissfully asleep. But she was not. Still, there was the slightest doubt, gnawing, niggling, refusing to let her rest. There was still the need to allay this hint of uneasiness. When all said and done, this was the man she loved. This was an extra special, irreplaceable person in her life. Abruptly, she leaped out of bed and dialed the number. The phone rang and rang. She hoped it was the right number, because she intended to let it ring, if need be, all night.

Henri was on one of those flat-bottomed boats which had been in vogue in the years immediately before the War. It was a beautiful Spring day, and the boat floated serenely along this, his favorite stretch of the river. There was an unreal silence as he dozed in the warm sunshine, miles from the nearest village. Now he could hear the faint melody of water rushing over a distant weir. As the boat drew nearer, the melody became a soothing overture. But underneath the melody was a discordant note. It became louder, and insistent, and oppressive, and eventually drowned out the music. Now, he could identify the raucous sound of jangling bells. The boat began to rock, gently at first, but soon with increasing vigor. Suddenly....Henri woke up. It was a telephone. The sound was coming in via the window, so kindly opened earlier by private Lens. It must be from James' office. But why didn't he answer it? And who could be calling at this hour?

With some difficulty he lifted himself off the bunk and peered through the window. The office light was on; the office door was open; the external switch had been operated. Something was wrong. He called softly. "Hello". There was, to Henri's dismay, no reply from Lens. He switched on the light. The other bunk was empty. Dressing as quickly as his condition would allow, he switched off the light and, taking his crutches, he hobbled cautiously towards the office. The living quarters were unoccupied. He picked up the phone. "Hello".

"Henri?" Charlotte's voice was tense, all the more so as she had expected to hear James.   "Where is James?"

"I don't know. He's not in his room"

"Henri. He's in danger. Find him! Help him!" The waves had returned.

"How do you know?"

"I know. I know. Find him, Henri. Please help him. Hurry!" She was becoming hysterical

"I will call you back very soon. Don't worry. He'll be OK". Henri replaced the receiver. He quickly searched the office. In one of the drawers of the desk he found the Luger. Fully loaded. Ready for action, as he was himself after the urgency of Charlotte's appeals. He took the gun and stood quite still. He could hear engines, aircraft engines. Getting closer. Strangest of all, he recognized the tone, a sound he had not heard for years. It was unmistakably a Caudron C440. A so-called Seagull. A twin-engine French military transport. The engines were being throttled back. It was going to land. What on earth could that be doing here?

James had recovered consciousness several minutes ago but had not let the German know. He heard the approaching aircraft but did not expect the bucket of cold water which was thrown over him. He was roughly pulled to his feet and dragged out of the door, the revolver held close to his head. They walked to the corner of the building while they waited for the aircraft to stop. James would have to take a chance very soon; once on the aircraft, he would be lost. Unobtrusively, he glanced at the office. The lights were out. Henri must be on the scene.
The aircraft came to a standstill. Without being told, James staggered towards the passenger door, which had now been opened from within. The engine idled, as James put as much distance between himself and the German as he could. As he reached the wingtip, he and the German were now in the full glare of the lights, James fell to the ground. Three shots rang out in quick succession, the sound partly obliterated by the noise of the engines. The German fell, dead, to the ground. James rolled under the wing and struggled to his feet. He ran, zig-zagging, into the shadow of the hangar. A soldier leapt from the aircraft, carrying a rifle. His life was ended by three more shots from Henri. The passenger door was hurriedly slammed and the engines gunned into full power. Thirty seconds later the plane was airborne. Within three minutes the sound of the engines had disappeared.
James walked to the bodies on the runway, his hands still secured behind his back. He was aware that Henri would be watching for any movement from the Germans. He approached with caution and kicked their weapons away. There was no movement. They were dead.

Five minutes later, James and Henri were in the office.
"She just said I was in danger? She didn't say how she knew?"
"That's right, mon ami".
James picked up the phone and dialed the number for Bishop's Lodge. It rang once before he heard Charlotte's voice.
"Hello CC. It's all right. There's nothing to worry about.
"Oh James. Thank God. What happened?"
"There was a minor incident, but it's OK now. We're both OK. I'll tell you about it when I see you. Go to sleep now, darling. Good night CC. I

love you". James replaced the receiver and walked into his private office. He looked at his reflection in the mirror. His mind was in turmoil. Was it possible? Could she really have known? Of one thing he was certain. She had saved his life.

Chapter 11

00.30 hours Calais Luftwaffe Base

Anton Oblat dozed in the staff car parked outside the office of the base Commanding Officer. It had been a hectic day, and not just because of the Allied invasion, which had <u>not</u> been thrown back into the sea in the first few hours, as promised by the German High Command. A roar of laughter from the still animated officer's mess startled him into consciousness. Fully alert now, he could see through a gap in the curtaining that Stockhausen was talking on the phone. He was obviously in a happy, relaxed and confident mood, a far cry from the tension of the last few weeks, and, in particular, of the last twenty-four hours.

Gradually, the sound of aircraft engines became audible. If it were the plane that he and Stockhausen were waiting for, it would have French markings, and would have been picked up on radar. The anti-aircraft batteries in the vicinity had been ordered not to open fire on a single aircraft. Maybe the phone call which had caused Stockhausen such glee had been a report of the approach of this plane. It was now overhead and circling; there was no doubt it was going to land. Oblat assumed this must be the plane carrying the English agent who had caused so much anguish to his boss. Stockhausen had been obsessed with this matter for weeks. He had been irritable and unpredictable. If this problem could be solved tonight, so much the better.

The S.S. Commander was now standing by the car, a strange, malicious anticipation etched into his features. The plane taxied along the runway and came to a halt about twenty yards from where the staff car was parked. The pilot killed the engine but remained in the cockpit. The silence was complete. Anton felt a slight ripple of unease; Stockhausen was smiling expectantly. After a few endless moments the passenger door was opened. Three of Stockhausen's own S.S. troops, hand-picked by him for this mission, climbed down. With their heads lowered and their arms hanging by their side, they stood forlornly on the tarmac. No prisoner emerged. For what seemed an eternity Stockhausen glared at them. The presence of a dozen Luftwaffe personnel probably saved their lives at that moment. Anton sat motionless in the driver's seat, staring directly ahead. He could not believe they had had the courage to return after failing in this particular mission. Stockhausen climbed into the back seat of the car mumbling incoherently. "...Calais...", the only audible word in a snarled order.

The journey took just over one hour, during which time Stockhausen rambled continuously. After several minutes Anton summoned up the courage to peek momentarily into the rear-view mirror, which was so positioned that he could see his boss. The reflection he saw of Stockhausen curdled his blood. His eyes were those of a demented, enraged man. The veins on his forehead bulged. It was as if he had been pushed beyond some limit, propelled into insanity

Chapter 12

17.30 hours Friday 23rd June Holmbury Base

It had been a hectic day. Since 7am raw recruits and experienced soldiers had been arriving, mainly singly or in twos. Luckily, all the non-commissioned officers and the ancillary staff had arrived before any of the combat soldiers, so that a blueprint for the organization of the base had been quickly established. Thankfully, the raw recruits were in a small minority, and James decided that they should start to learn parade-ground drill, the basis of discipline and team spirit, at once. Immediately on arrival they had been formed into platoons, with new people added as they arrived. For hours they had marched up and down the parade ground, responding as best they could to the orders, quick-march, left-right, about-turn, left-wheel, right-wheel, attention, stand easy, present arms, screamed almost incoherently at them by the sergeants. By dusk the NCOs were able to report that good progress was being made.

Sir Charles' car arrived at about 8.30pm. He had been disturbed to hear of the attempt to abduct James and had ordered a full inquiry. He had been even more surprised to hear of the part played by his daughter in frustrating the attempt. This meeting with James was partly to decide, in advance of their weekend at Bishop's Lodge, how they would handle the inevitable questions from Charlotte. They agreed that, for the duration of the war, it was still necessary to protect her from full knowledge of James' 'other duties', and that the story they had told her so far, about 'Coastal Command', was still feasible, and did not need to be changed. The problem was, what to tell her in future. Above all, it was crucial not to let her know that James was a particular target for a senior SS officer, as it was common knowledge that the SS had enormous resources and were fanatically single-minded in their vendettas. This might alarm her almost as much as it did James. They decided they would stick to the story of the training program, which had the advantage of being true, although it was not the whole truth, and that if there were any further examples of 'this mental hocus-pocus', as Sir Charles called it, they would have to deal with each incident as it arose. They would put the recent events down to a case of mistaken identity, and tell Charlotte, with sufficient lack of clarity due to 'security', that the SS had seemed to believe that a major political figure, transparently, from the description they would give her, Churchill, had been visiting the base. Examples of misinformation like this were commonplace during wartime. In any case, the war would surely be over within twelve months, so the need for secrecy would soon be less pressing than previously.

At 9.30 they set off for a weekend at Bishop's Lodge. Neither spoke during the hour-long journey, each being immersed in his own thoughts. Sir Charles, still skeptical of his daughter's highly developed 'sixth sense', was disturbed about the serious breach of security that had taken place; he was beginning to believe that there was a spy, or at least a German sympathizer, at the War Office, probably in a fairly junior position, but, with proper training and boldness, still able to manipulate situations. It was unlikely that the outcome of the War could be altered by these treacherous activities, but he felt that many losses and much damage could be caused if his fears were correct.

James' thoughts revolved around Charlotte. Her phone call had saved his life, there was no doubt about that. He knew that she would not expect any sort of reward for this; his own safety would be prize enough for her. But if she *could* sense his danger, and if she had done so on the numerous occasions in the past when she had claimed to do so, then she must have endured intolerable trauma. He owed it to her to avoid danger in the future if possible, but before any conclusions could be drawn or any decisions made, they needed to talk.

15.00 hours. Saturday 24th June Bishops Lodge

They sat in deckchairs, basking in the blazing heat of the sun. The last of the lemonade had gone, but she knew there was plenty of beer in the cellar, although she also knew that he would not want to drink alcohol until after her father returned from visiting friends. She sat patiently, waiting for James to frame a question that would elicit a response that he could cope with.

"Yes, darling. But, what *kind* of feeling?" It was the same question, but with different words.

"All I can say is that sometimes there is a sudden, unexpected, unexplainable feeling of....". Now, she was using the same words "...fear, depression, foreboding, dread, as if something terrible is happening. Sometimes strong, sometimes not so strong. It comes and goes for no reason I can tell you, but the one consistent thing is that I always feel you are in some sort of danger or need some sort of help. And then," she snapped her fingers, "it just vanishes. That's why I call it 'the waves'. It comes and goes like....waves!" She was pleased that this was, at last, being taken seriously.

He looked at her with an uncomprehending expression. She continued. "Darling, the proof is there. This time, I was able to phone you, and we know what happened". She had accepted the story concocted by her father and James

"Yes. Your intervention made a difference, there's no doubt about that. I have to accept what you say at face value. But, where does it leave us?"

"Well, it doesn't leave us anywhere. It makes no difference, really. Most of the time I can't contact you. But, if there is trouble, I will know. It's just there, a fact of life".

James was amazed that she could sit there and accept this incredible, mysterious thing as if it were just a matter of routine, which, in fact, to her, it was. Charlotte continued "Why should it be such a big deal? It's not as if anything can be done about it. It's not an illness it's just....a fact".

"I'm concerned because I don't want you to put up with nightmares whenever I'm....", he wished he had said 'if ever', " in trouble. We are all 'in trouble' at some time, and usually it is just nothing important."

"James. My darling James". She was smiling at him now, that warm, kind, generous smile that had first won his heart. "We've talked about this for hours, and it seems that it only happens when you're in extreme circumstances, not the run of the mill air-raid or other...inconveniences of war. It'll probably be less in the future, now that you are just doing training, important though that is." She smiled again, pleased at his concern, and that he had accepted, finally, what she had said for so long.

'...only doing training...' The words sliced through him like a scalpel. For the remaining months of the War he may well spend all his time in training. That would be fine. But he had to face the fact that he may well be called upon to undertake hazardous missions. He leaned over and kissed her, but, for once, she was not the main subject of his thoughts. He smiled at her, but his gentleness concealed a steely resolve. Whatever the consequences, he would refuse to be part of any further hazardous operations.

Chapter 13

20.00 hours Tuesday 15th August Holmbury Base

A sudden, unexpected and definitely unseasonal downpour had turned an exercise which should have taken three hours into one which took five. James was satisfied with the progress of the troops under his command. They were acting as a team, a vital aspect of good soldiering, and he felt that he had won their respect, although it was unlikely that he would actually lead them into battle at any stage. He was surprised, given the late hour, to find the orderly still at his desk.

"Strict instructions to pass on this telephone message to you personally, Sir". It was a message from Sir Charles to the effect that James should join him at Bishops' Lodge the coming weekend.

"Call Sir Charles' office first thing tomorrow, and tell him that his instructions have been received. Thank you for staying on until my return. Good night". With this James stood to one side to allow the orderly to pass.

Saturday 19th August Bishops' Lodge

Charlotte had recently volunteered as a nursing auxiliary at the local hospital, and, being on duty until the evening, was not at home when James arrived at lunchtime. Sir Charles showed him in and invited him to take the chair opposite his own in the study.

"James, some intelligence reports, those of fairly low grade in terms of secrecy, are routinely circulated to relevant base commanders above a certain rank. You won't have received any, but I receive them every week". He placed a briefcase on the desk and took out a file. "This file contains the latest batch I have received. There is nothing in here which is of such importance that it's general dissemination would be a threat to national security. Be that as it may, if I were to show you these reports, that would be a court-martial offence. If you looked at them without permission, that would be a court-martial offence. If I merely *discussed* the contents of any report with you, that would be a court-martial offence". Sir Charles stood up, leaving the file on the desk.

"I order you to protect these files from interference during my absence for the next hour or so". With that, Sir Charles left the room. A few moments later James heard the front door slam. He looked out of the window in time to see Sir Charles, with the dog walking freely by his side, stroll to the end of the drive and out through the gates.

James had not spoken since he had entered the study. He sat down at the desk and looked at the file. Obviously, there was something in the files that Sir Charles wanted him to know. He picked up the file and took out the contents. There were seven reports, each one marked 'confidential', the lowest security rating.

The first concerned German naval plans. It was graded 'UNRELIABLE', which meant it was an unconfirmed report from one, less-reliable source only. The second would have been of interest to his brother, Simon. In fact, it was probably known to Simon. It stated that on 11th August the test launch had taken place of Ruhrstahl X-4 rocket-propelled missile. It was designed for use by the new ME 262 fighter-bomber, and had reached a speed of over 1000 mph. The report was graded 'RELIABLE', being from a known, trusted source, and confirmed by another known, trusted source, independent of the first. James whistled silently at the thought of a missile travelling at 1000 mph. He thanked God that these things take months to produce in large numbers. He had to hand it to the Germans; whatever the madness of their leaders, they were second to none in the fields of innovation and research.

The third report was the one intended for James' attention. It read as follows;

CONFIDENTIAL FILE No. 2070272 DATE Recd. 120844
GRADE; RELIABLE/UNCONFIRMED.

ON 10th AUGUST UNITS OF THE WEHRMACHT STATIONED IN THE CALAIS AREA ATTEMPTED TO DESERT. SS TROOPS THWARTED THIS ACTION, BUT OTHER UNITS OF THE WEHRMACHT TURNED ON THE SS. LOCAL SS COMMANDER, STURMBANNFUEHRER STOCKHAUSEN AND ENTOURAGE MASSACRED. OTHER SS UNITS RESTORED ORDER. RECOMMENDATION; NO ACTION.

James replaced all the files. That was obviously the one he had been meant to see. So, Stockhausen was dead, killed by his own side. James felt no joy, no pleasure, no relief, no victory. But he was filled with a feeling of safety.

Charlotte and Sir Charles arrived in her car. Obviously, Sir Charles had walked to the hospital and met her there. "Yes, lieutenant?" These were Sir Charles first words. Charlotte was surprised at the formality but put it down to some male interplay of no importance.

"Yes, Colonel". James' words answered Sir Charles unasked question and closed the subject forever.

"What about auxiliary nurse Crayne? Doesn't she get a mention?"

James kissed her as Sir Charles moved to switch on the radio. "It's six o' clock.
Time for the news."

The news was about the heavy bombardment of London by the V-1 'pilotless planes', already nicknamed 'doodlebug', which had begun on the night of 12/13 August. Sir Charles had often expressed concern over the secret weapons that Hitler had boasted about. The newscaster announced that it was believed that these new weapons were being launched from sites in the area around Calais. James and Sir Charles made a point of not looking at each other.

Chapter 14
15.00 hours Wednesday 30th August Kent

As a sympathizer with the British Union of Fascists since that Party was founded in 1932, John Perkins had agreed to take a low profile in its political campaigning. He was left in no doubt that his role was destined to be one of active service, and he had agreed to make himself available on this basis.

After the outbreak of war, with the dissolution of the Party, he had been contacted by the last remaining underground elements of British fascists and agreed that he would be of use in the cause of British fascism. He did not feel that this was unpatriotic. Indeed, it was the politicians who were unpatriotic. It was they who had promised a 'land fit for heroes' following the carnage of the First World War. Instead, the ordinary British working man found only unemployment and poverty. His own efforts since 1932 were intended to replace the current political elite with one more sensitive to the needs of ordinary people, and if this required military interference from abroad, so be it. The blitz on London and other cities was the price that had to be paid to achieve these goals, just as had been the case in Spain some years previously, when General Franco was brought to power. If he had one regret in recent months it was that he had not been able to inform his contacts of the details of the Normandy invasion. He had been in the wrong place at the wrong time.

Now, he had received fairly odd instructions, not for the first time, but agreed to carry them out without question. Initially, he had been concerned that the village was so small that his presence would be noticed, but the frequency of his visits over last four weeks had made him almost part of the scenery. This was a good thing, because today was the main event.

"Still not got it fixed yet?" It was the grocer's wife, a simple, friendly soul, a salt of the earth, British yeoman's wife, one of those he was originally interested in helping. Yet, politically naive.

"Not yet, love. Should have it done today".

"I bet you'll be glad."

"Not really. If it's not this one, it'll be another one. It's all the same to me".

She smiled pleasantly and went back into the shop. He took his equipment from the van and strapped himself into the safety harness. Securing this to his satisfaction, he ascended the wooden telegraph pole. Settling himself as comfortably as possible, he tapped into the wire which he had identified on previous visits as the one which connected the Commando base nearby to the outside world. It was 3.15pm. The call was due at 3.30. All he had to do was wait.

15.30 hours Office of Colonel Charles Crayne

It was just after 3.30 when the intercom buzzed.

"Yes".

"Call for you, Sir, from colonel Tuffnel at Woodvale barracks, near Ramsgate".

Sir Charles picked up the receiver. "Hello colonel. Colonel Charles Crayne here".

"Sorry to bother you, old chap. This is Tuffnel here, CO at Woodvale. I've got a couple of your chaps here, seem to have been on some sort of mission. Arrived here last night in need of some minor first aid and a good meal. They say they have some urgent information which they refuse to divulge except to you, in person. I don't mind telling you I was a bit put out, but I know you chaps do some cloak-and-dagger stuff and so I didn't press them. Unfortunately, one of them can't move because he's got a broken ankle. Do you think you could come over tonight and de-brief them? They did say their info is quite important.

"What are their names?"

"We have a private Taylor and a lance corporal Scott".

Sir Charles recognized the names. They had been missing for months following their last mission into occupied France.

"I'll call you back shortly". He replaced the receiver and spoke into the intercom. "How long would it take to get to Woodvale?".

After a few moments the orderly replied, "About two hours, Sir".

"Get me Woodvale on the phone".

It took the orderly only a few moments to make the connection. "Woodvale barracks. Can I help you".

"Can I speak to colonel Tuffnel please. This is colonel Crayne".

"One moment please". Perkins covered the mouthpiece with his hand to conceal the noise of a passing train. This was just the kind of thing that might give the game away. There was a chance, minor indeed, but a chance none the less that Crayne might see the train and connect in his mind the background sounds he heard on the phone with the sights he was seeing. When the train had passed Perkins continued. "Colonel Tuffnel has left the office for a few moments. Will you hold?" At the top of the telegraph pole Perkins held his breath.

Sir Charles knew that a few moments often turned into several minutes.

"No. Just tell him to expect me at about 8.30. He'll know what it's about".

"Certainly, Sir. Thank you". His part in the plot was now complete. He had impersonated a British orderly in order to lure a British officer away from his base. Hardly war-winning stuff, but never mind; we all have only a small part in a bigger picture. He disconnected his equipment and descended the telegraph pole. There was just enough time for a cup of tea before filling in his time sheet to indicate that he had completed his last job at 2.00pm, which fact could easily be verified, but had been held up for more than an hour by a military convoy, which fact could be neither confirmed nor refuted.

Sir Charles glanced through the files of private Taylor and lance corporal Scott. There was nothing to indicate that they had been in a position to learn important information, but it was unwise to ignore any possibilities.

At six o' clock he climbed into the back seat of the staff car for the journey to Woodvale. It would be impossible for anyone to contact him for at least two hours.

Chapter 15

16.00 hours Weds 30th August The War Office London

Sergeant Baker was not amused. He had been due to go off duty in a few minutes until, in a flurry of signals, he had been ordered to drive over to Holmbury and collect a lieutenant Courtney and bring him to the

War Office. What a pain. Well, they could just wait until he had finished his tea. In any case, he was due to pick him up at 5.00pm sharp, so he reckoned he had a little time to spare.

16.45 hours Holmbury Base

James was perusing some files in his office when the telephone rang. "Hello".

"Is that Lieutenant Courtney?"

"Speaking".

"Sir, this is Captain Anderson, attached to the War Office. I'm phoning you from there now. I am instructed to inform you that you are required to attend a meeting at the War Office. You are to meet a Mr. Wright. A car will arrive in a few minutes to bring you here. Sir, this is a matter of extreme urgency and you are to come as you are. It will not be necessary to collect any clothing or equipment".

"Captain Anderson, this is very irregular..."

"I realize that, Sir, but I assure you this is of the utmost importance".

"Very well. I shall leave as soon as the car arrives".

"Thank you, Sir".

James replaced the receiver and wondered what all this could be about. At that moment the intercom buzzed.

"Yes?".

"Sir, there's a Sgt. Baker here to drive you to London, Sir".

"I'll be with him in a moment". James scribbled down the names of the sergeant, captain and official who were involved in this, and gave a brief account of what had happened to his orderly. "This is where I'll be if you need to contact me". With that, he left in the company of the sergeant. The latter, it transpired, was equally in the dark.

They arrived at the War Office shortly after 6.00pm. Most of the staff had left, but the guard at the entrance had been informed of James' arrival, and directed him to an office on the second floor. Sergeant Baker was informed that he would not be needed and that he could go off duty. On the second floor James followed the signs indicating the interview room in which he was to meet Mr. Wright. As he walked along the corridor he could hear muted sounds of typewriters, and it dawned on him how different were people's experience of the War. The walls were a dull cream color, and the air was heavy with the smell of floor polish. He soon found the room he was seeking. He knocked on the door, and a voice from within invited him to enter.

"Lieutenant Courtney, or would you prefer to be called 'Hotel'? Please sit down and thank you for coming at such short notice. Sir Charles assured me you would be available in an emergency". Mr.

Wright spoke with a slight Scottish accent. He was in his mid-fifties and looked every inch a civil servant. "The matter I have to discuss with you is so urgent that we must get down to business straight away. Do you know what operation FUSE is?"

"No".

"It is an American scientific/military program to develop an atomic bomb. Do you know what an atomic bomb is?"

"No". James was amazed that such information could be given so freely. There must be something very serious going on.

"Well, neither do I, because I'm not a scientist. I'm a War Office staffer and all we know is what the boffins tell us. And what they tell us is that a single atomic bomb would obliterate the whole of London in a few moments". He paused to allow James to absorb the magnitude of what he had said. "Operation FUSE is nearing completion. The Americans are sure that they will have a bomb ready in a few months. Needless to say, the Germans have also been doing research in the same field, and we have received, in the last 24 hours, reliable, confirmed information that they have completed the building of a bomb which they intend to use shortly against London, in an attempt to force us to negotiate, or face further similar attacks".

"How long is 'shortly'?"

"We don't know, but it could be imminent. The V1 attacks have enabled them to test their ability to deliver the bomb. We're starting to shoot them down now, but we know they have other means of delivery which are much less vulnerable". James thought of the intelligence report he had seen at Bishop's Lodge; a rocket-propelled missile, travelling at 1000 mph.

Wright continued, "What we need to do is knock out the launching sites. We are fairly sure they can't launch from a distance of more than about 200 miles, and we know that the number of suitable locations is limited. We need to investigate the most likely places, and if we find the launching site, we'll bomb it and send in airborne Commandos to finish the job. Hopefully, that will give us enough time to defeat the Nazis and finish the War. It takes months to build a sophisticated installation for launching large missiles, and in a few months, with France, Belgium and the Netherlands liberated, Germany itself would be too far for them to attack London". Again, he paused for James' thoughts to catch up. "We've identified a site in the area near Calais that needs to be looked at. You've been in Calais several times, and you know the terrain and the Resistance well. We want you to go there and have a look around".

"What exactly would I be looking for?"

"You're an experienced man, and you've seen all sorts of installations. You'll be looking for a *new* type of installation, different from anything else you've seen, camouflaged, obviously, to conceal it from aerial intelligence, heavily fortified, heavily guarded. Unusual; look for new railway tracks that don't seem to go anywhere, of a different gauge from the normal. Roads with signs of scorching. Anything, *anything,* out of the ordinary. You'll be unarmed and posing as a French peasant, with genuine French papers. Just get in, have a look around, and if you think it's a candidate, just let us know through the normal Resistance channels, and we'll bomb it to Hell and back. Arrangements will be made with the local resistance to get you back in a couple of days, whether you find anything or not. A quick job, low risk, in and out, pronto".

"And when do you want this done?"

"We want you to leave here now and be in Calais in three hours. The Resistance has been informed and it's all set up. Couple of days; minimum risk, but highest priority, given what's at stake".

James thought for a moment. "I'm usually briefed by Sir Charles Crayne before I go on a mission. Do you mind if I call him?"

"Certainly. Use this phone".

James dialed the number of Sir Charles' office. Wright knew it would be a wasted call.

"Can I speak to Sir Charles. please".

"He's not here at the moment. Can I take a message?".
James recognized the voice of the orderly at the other end of the line.
"When do you expect him back?".

"Not until very late this evening".

"Thank you. There is no message. Just tell him I called. This is Lieutenant Courtney; it's nothing important". James dialed the number for Bishops' Lodge. Charlotte was in the shower, unable to hear it. James addressed Wright. "Isn't it better to use the French Resistance"? Wright picked up a folder. "I would have thought so". He took a single piece of paper out of the folder and laid it on the desk so that he could read it. From his position, seeing the paper upside down, James noted the words 'Downing Street' at the top. "But I have here a letter, delivered to me by hand this morning, instructing me, quote 'to take the most immediate and reliable action' in this matter". He looked at James with a raised eyebrow. "I have orders from the highest authority." Again, he paused. "It might be of interest to you that, if you accept these orders, and you don't have to, you will be the sixteenth agent going in tonight".

"There's no question of not accepting the orders. I'm as ready as I can be".

"Thank you, lieutenant". Wright passed an envelope to James. "In here are your orders and some notes of guidance about what to look for. I expect you'll be back by Saturday at the latest, and whether you find anything or not, please send me a report as soon as possible, as snippets of information from several sources all add to the bigger picture. Once again, thank you. And good hunting".

Wright pressed a button, and within a few moments a young man in uniform entered the office. "Take the lieutenant to the car, please". With a final handshake, James left the office. A few minutes later he was on his way to an unnamed airfield in East Anglia. The young man informed him it was a two-hour drive. It was a few minutes past 7 o'clock.

Mr. Wright saw James get into the car from a window in the interview room. He returned to his desk and dialed a number. The ringing tone sounded once before it was answered. There were no words from the person at the other end. "All is as planned". He leaned back in his chair to review the situation. He guessed that the Americans were developing a bomb similar to the type that the Germans were working on, but he did not know the name of the project, which, in fact, was the Manhattan Project, but 'Operation FUSE' sounded OK. Certainly, it had convinced Courtney, who was now on his way, as a dutiful British soldier, to an uncertain future. It was amazing how a clerical employee, with minimal authority, could manipulate situations within a large bureaucratic system; he was constantly startled at the ease with which he, a sympathizer and friend to Germany, was able to give orders to British officers, and to make arrangements using British military resources. So long as he did not become too ambitious, it required only a piece of notepaper, apparently official, and a signature, and one other thing, namely, the most powerful item in the British Army. And that, or at least one of them, he had concealed about his person. He took it from his pocket and gazed at it, smiling. It weighed only a few ounces, was cheap and easy to replace, and yet it was a priceless asset in his work. It was a War Office rubber stamp, to reproduce the word 'Official'. Without a rubber stamp, nothing in the British Army could move; with it, the whole Army could be manipulated.

He put it back in his pocket and contemplated the blank wall opposite. A thought occurred to him. Was there in German High Command a minor official working for the British, feeding information to the Allies and disinformation to the Germans; concealing the whereabouts of Resistance fighters or downed pilots? If so, that man or woman would be a mirror image of himself. He smiled at the thought.

Chapter 16

21.00 hours Woodvale Barracks

Sir Charles sent for the orderly, but every answer he gave only confirmed what Colonel Tuffnel had said. "Sir, we didn't get a single telephone call all day. And we didn't make any to the best of my knowledge. With respect, Sir, are you sure it was Woodvale, and not Wood Valley? We sometimes get calls directed here that are meant for Wood Valley". The orderly was genuine in his suggestion, so Sir Charles controlled his irritation.

"No, it was definitely Woodvale, and definitely, the call was, supposedly, from Colonel Tuffnel. Thank you, Corporal".

Colonel Tuffnel dismissed the orderly. "Well, I'm sorry, old chap. It looks like a practical joke, and not a very good one".

Sir Charles looked at Tuffnel. He was Welsh, with an accent totally different from the man he had spoken to earlier in the day. "Colonel, may I use the telephone?" The request was a mere formality.

"Do you think it might be something more sinister than a joke?" Sir Charles nodded in reply.

"Please, be my guest. Do you need any of my staff?"

"No, thank you very much".

Calm, lucid thinking was what was needed now. It seemed that he had been deliberately lured away from his base. But why? And who could have used the names of two of his missing agents, Taylor and Scott? What were the possibilities? If there were to be an attempt to assassinate him, it could surely have been carried out at his base just as easily as anywhere else. There had been no incident en route to Woodvale. He quickly rejected the idea. The first thing to do was to contact his own base and find out if anything unusual had happened.

Two minutes later Sir Charles replaced the receiver. 'Very quiet, Sir', the orderly had said. Only one phone call had been received all afternoon, from Lieutenant Courtney, and no message left. Obviously, it had been an unimportant matter. It was 21.20 hours.

Sir Charles sat with his eyes closed, in deep concentration. Somewhere, there must be a clue, some insignificant incident that might help to throw some light onto this bizarre affair. He decided to call Holmbury. Perhaps James, with a clear mind, could see something that he, Sir Charles, had overlooked.

The orderly who answered the phone recognized Sir Charles' voice immediately and informed him of the events of that afternoon. Sir Charles replaced the receiver and held his chin. James had left the base at about 5 o'clock. One hour to London, perhaps one hour for the meeting, and one hour back. He could, should, have been back at 8.00, but he was not, and it was now past 9.30.

He called Bishops' Lodge. To avoid alarming Charlotte he made small talk for a few minutes, and then asked when James was to come over.

"Two weeks on Saturday. Why?"

"Just checking my diary so there are no overlaps. See you later".

She had not said that James was there now. He was not at his base, so, where was he? A call to Simon, in case James had taken the opportunity of being in London to visit his brother.

"Simon, this is Sir Charles. How are you, my boy?"

"Sir Charles, what a surprise. I'm fine. How are you?"

"Oh, bearing up, you know. Tell me, Simon, has James been in touch with you today?"

"No. I've been here since 6.30 and there have been no callers".

"Simon, one of my officers is going on a mission tonight, and I've left the file in my office. How can I find out which airfield he'll be flying from?" Sir Charles was beginning to become uneasy about James' whereabouts. It was unlikely that there was anything amiss, but just for his own satisfaction, Sir Charles wanted to be sure that there was nothing to be concerned about.

"All flights are coordinated by controllers at Biggin Hill, but they aren't likely to give information over the phone".

"Well, I'll give them a call anyway. Thank you, Simon. You must get over to Bishops' Lodge soon".

"Thank you, Sir Charles. I'll look forward to that. Goodnight".

Sir Charles had a high-ranking friend in the R.A.F, a man he had known from his schooldays. He looked at his watch; 9.45. He hoped his friend was at home.

"Hello Teddy. Charlie here. How goes it with the poor bloody Air Force?"

"Charlie. How are you, old man."

"Hanging on grimly, at my age. Listen Teddy, will you do me a favor?"

"If I can, I'm sure I will".

"Will you phone your chaps at Biggin Hill, the ones who co-ordinate the flights, and find out if any of my boys are going behind enemy lines tonight, and if there are, can you find out as much information as possible and call me back here? And Teddy, this is a bit urgent". Sir Charles gave his friend the telephone number of Woodvale.

"Righto. I'll call you back in a few minutes". It was 10.05.

He checked the parachute again. It was properly secured. The intercom sounded, and James heard the pilot's voice telling him that they were approaching the target area. They had encountered no enemy action at all, which was as expected for a lone aircraft. James knew that there was hardly any wind, despite the rush of air over the wings, so the conditions were perfect for a parachutist. With just a small amount of luck he would land exactly on target. He got himself into a position to jump as soon as the pilot switched on the green light. He looked at his watch; 10pm.

"Yes, it was ordered very late this afternoon. A very last-minute job. Someone is going in over Calais. I don't know who it is, or the objective. I don't even know if it's one of your boys".

"Teddy, for something to be arranged that quickly without my knowledge it must have been a very high authorization, maybe even Joint Chiefs. Do you agree?"

"I would say so, old man".

Sir Charles hesitated for a moment. "Teddy, I want you to countermand the order and bring the plane back, along with the officer. I'll take full responsibility. Colonel Tuffnel is present to witness that I have made this request."

Sir Charles looked at Tuffnel, whose face betrayed utter astonishment. The idea of countermanding an order from the Joint Chiefs, or anyone else, for that matter, was completely foreign to his experience.

Teddy was equally nonplussed. "Charlie, are you sure?"

"Teddy, please do it. Phone me back here with confirmation as soon as".

"As you wish." The phone went dead.

Tense moments passed, as Sir Charles paced the office. Tuffnel stood motionless, unable to comprehend what he had just witnessed. Finally, after what seemed a lifetime, the phone rang. Even in his shell-shocked condition Tuffnel was able to answer. "It's for you, Sir Charles".

"Charlie, Teddy here. Sorry, old boy. Too late. Your man had jumped a few minutes before we got through. If there's anything I can do..."

"No, thanks Teddy. I'll take care of things. Thanks very much. Will be in touch soon. Good night." He replaced the receiver and asked that his car be brought to the office. Thanking Colonel Tuffnel for his help, Sir Charles took his leave. It was to be a somber, silent trip back to his base. Possibly, maybe, after all, it might not be James, but he had a heavy feeling in the pit of his stomach.

The sound of the engine grew weaker, until, at last, it disappeared altogether. This was one of James' favorite sensations; adrenalin coursing through his veins, senses heightened, and yet with the silence came a complete lack of discernible stress. For a few brief moments he could enjoy this feeling before he would have to scrutinize the landing area, as best he could in the gloom, for possible hazards. He landed safely, quickly freed himself from the harness and buried the parachute. Everything was running well. He had a good feeling about this mission. He would make his way to the farm and get a few hours' sleep before meeting his Resistance contacts at 6.00am.

The night was mild and still. The Moon gave sufficient light for him to get his bearings quickly. All the landmarks were there; the mill, the footbridge, like some eternal monuments. Memories flooded back of the missions he had been involved in, the blows he had struck against the madmen who thought that armed aggression was a legitimate instrument of national policy. His body tingled with the thrill of excitement he knew so well. Really, he was lucky. The Free World must be full of men who, outraged that a nation should rise up and destroy the homes and lives of its neighbors and the peace of the World, would willingly take the chance to attack the beast in its lair. But it was he, James Courtney, who had that chance.

How he detested the Nazis. It seemed incredible that there were people in positions of power in national governments who had somehow missed the universal debate on the waste and futility of war. It was incomprehensible to James that a man with the views of Hitler could seduce a nation and bring war to the World. Certainly, the aftermath of the First World War had been difficult for the Germans, and the Western democracies were at fault for imposing such harsh conditions. But things had improved in the mid-thirties. Why then had they felt the need to embark on a policy of military conquest? Had they not learned the lessons of history? And now, the greatest obscenity; a weapon that could devastate whole cities, and thousands of people, in a matter of moments. What could be in the minds of people who would develop such an instrument? He hoped it *would* be in the Calais area, and that he would have a hand in its destruction. But he must put these thoughts out of his mind and concentrate on matters at hand. It was a two-mile trek across open countryside to the farm, slightly less than an hour.

He had made good time, as there had been no patrols to delay him. He could see Sophie's farm, but the expected light was not illuminated. Perhaps candles were in short supply, in these harsh times. He thought it strange that he had heard no bombers on their way with packages of retribution for the Germans. The words of Mr. Wright came back to him. 'Attack may be imminent'. Perhaps it was already too late. Maybe London had been attacked in the last hour, and death and confusion reigned. There was nothing he could do about it. He put the thought out of his mind. Tomorrow would be his chance. By late afternoon he would have a good idea if there was anything sinister in the area. By 8pm London would know. By midnight the bombers would be sent, and he would be on his way home. He imagined that, for something as important as this, the area would be saturated with high explosives for three or four hours. Then, there would be a lull, before thousands of Commandos would be sent in just before dawn. The area would be isolated and they would dispose of all German military personnel and blow up all equipment and installations in the vicinity. He thought of Sir Charles, even now poring over maps planning, organizing. And he knew Sir Charles would be thinking of him. That must be the reason he could not contact him earlier; he must have been in conference all day.

From his position overlooking the farm he scanned the countryside. All was still and quiet. Cautiously, he approached the farmhouse. He felt the slight tug of something on his boot, followed by the sound, nearby, of some utensils or other items crashing to the floor. It sounded very loud in the stillness of the night, but he knew the noise would not travel far. And he knew it was her way of warning herself of the stealthy approach of someone unknown. He stood totally still, fully aware that by now, a gun would be trained on his chest. He made no attempt to conceal himself. To do so would invite a deadly response. He merely called out, in a low voice, "Sophie. It's Hotel". A few moments passed, presumably so that she could satisfy herself that it was indeed the British agent she had shared so many adventures with. Presently, he heard the sound of door bolts being drawn back.

"Welcome, my friend." A dim light was visible as she opened the door.

"Thank you, madam."

Most of his missions had involved a visit to this farm, since the time, four years earlier, when Henri had first brought him here. He saw again her dazzling smile, her soft blue eyes, her wavy, blond hair. She must be in her mid-forties, and she was still attractive. He wondered again how she must have looked in the first bloom of womanhood. He knew that her appearance concealed a courage and steely resolve that would be the envy of many men.

Their eyes met, and he felt the warmth and generosity of her affection "Thank you for taking Henri".

"So, it *was* you. I thought as much". To know that he had taken Henri back to England on the night of the disastrous raid on Foin she must have been on the scene when he had the fight with the German sentry. She walked over to a cupboard and picked up a large bottle labelled 'tanning fluid'. In fact, it was the best red wine to be had in this part of France, labelled as tanning fluid to put off any German who may want to steal it. She filled two small glasses and sipped before replying.

"When you didn't return on time I realized something had gone wrong, but I saw you return to the beach. I continually flashed your code sign so that the men who came to pick you up would stay as long as possible, and we know the rest. I saw everything that happened".

"Did you see Stockhausen?"

"Yes. He watched you sail away but spoke to no-one".
James allowed himself a wry smile.

"Tomorrow, we'll talk more, but I must arise early". With this, he stood up and went to her bedroom. She had long ago decided that a good nights' sleep was more important for him than for her. Accordingly, she insisted that he have the bed, while she slept on the sofa. Relaxed and confident, James soon fell into a deep sleep.

He drifted into and out of Charlotte's dreams that night, a smile here, a gesture there. She slept peacefully, blissfully unaware of the catastrophe which would engulf him over the next 48 hours.

Midday Thursday 31st August 1944 The War Office.

It was always the same. In every historical account of every war in which Britain had become involved that he had read about since his schooldays, the British were never prepared, with the possible exception of the Spanish Armada. They always got a bloody nose at first, came back with overwhelming resources and, more often than not, gave a good account of themselves. Another notable exception, he mused, was the American War of Independence. He anticipated that there would be growing complacency within the civil authorities, as the Allies pushed further into France and then into Germany itself, and victory was in sight. Sir Charles was in no doubt that the Allies would win the war, barring the appearance of the 'Wonder Weapons' about which Hitler had so often bragged, especially the so-called Atom bomb. And he was equally certain that Russia would get most from the peace negotiations. In the geographic and military/political situation which would develop in the decade after the War, it would not surprise him in the least if Germany were in a better economic condition than Britain, such was the complacency and smugness of the English ruling class.

He could detect it even now; inertia. Nobody could be bothered. He had phoned the War Office and told them he wanted, as a matter of urgency, authorization to carry out an inquiry, low-level, not too many waves, just to satisfy himself that everything was in proper order. All he wanted to do was interview a Sgt. Baker, Capt. Anderson, and a Mr. Wright.

"Sir Charles, it will be awkward to say the least to get hold of these people in a hurry. Mr. Wright is not in the office today, and Captain Anderson is on a long weekend leave, and is not due back until next

Tuesday. As for Sergeant Baker, I do not even know who he is". The official did not want to refuse. He just did not want the inconvenience.

"But if it were important enough, you would be able to get hold of them in a few hours, wouldn't you"? Sir Charles was exercising all his patience.

"Certainly, but we would need rather more than mere suspicions".

"And you could fairly easily find Sergeant Baker, couldn't you"?

"Well yes..."

Sir Charles had placed his cards on the table, well aware of the delaying and denying tactics which seemed just a game to these officials, except for the final Ace. "You see, the problem is this. If my 'mere suspicions' are correct, then it is likely that there is a German agent in the War Office, who is able, without proper authority, to authorize covert missions, and who may have access to all sorts of sensitive information. It's not a situation we should allow to continue for too long, don't you think?"

There was silence at the other end of the phone. "I'll call you back shortly, Sir Charles".

16.00 hours The War Office

Mr. Wright had been the first to arrive, as he lived closest to Whitehall. He had spent most of the morning on the local Common, taking the air and sunlight. He had arrived back at his lodgings to be told by his landlady that he was required to go to the War Office urgently. Security at reception had not been surprised to see him come in on his day off, having been warned to expect him. The spy concealed his irritation at the inability of the security man to throw any light on the mystery of why he had been summoned. He directed Mr. Wright to one of the offices on the top floor, where a secretary he had never seen before showed him into an ante-room. He was asked to wait until his name was announced over the intercom, and then enter into the main office, which she indicated. Within ten minutes, sergeant Baker arrived. Anxious to glean information, Wright immediately struck up conversation.

"How's the War going for you, then?"

"The War's going OK. It's just fagging up here to London that gets on your nerves".

"What, you have to come up here every week?".

"No, I've been here twice in my life, today and yesterday, and that's twice too often".

"Seems unusual. Important business, was it?" Wright hoped that his tone was not suspiciously inquisitive.

"I don't know. I had to drive some Commando officer up here as if the world depended on it. And now, up here again".

This was all the warning Mr. Wright needed. He left the ante-room and asked the secretary for directions to the men's room. Once outside the office, he headed straight for the front door.

"Leaving already, Mr. Wright?" The security man's tone was pleasant. He was not trying to prevent Mr. Wright from leaving the building, unusual though such a short visit to the Office was, and it would not be prudent of Wright to give him cause for suspicion. He could very quickly summon assistance, and even detain any person if he felt he should.

"Just popping out for some matches".

"I've got a light, Sir".

"Oh, well, I want a newspaper as well".

"Righto. Can you sign out, please."

"I will if you like, but I'll only be gone a minute." The security officer was dubious but decided to bend the rules.

"Alright. See you in a minute".

Once outside the building, Wright looked carefully around. No one suspicious could be seen, but he caught sight of a familiar figure walking along the road on the other side of the street towards the War Office. Wright bent down to tie his shoelace. The man started to cross the road; he was definitely heading for the War Office. Wright started to walk down the steps as the other man started to walk up. The man's identity and presence here, today, under these circumstances, was enough to convince Wright that his career as a German agent was over.

"Hello. Mr. Wright"

"Hello, Captain Anderson"

16.15 Hours.

Mr. Wright did not believe in coincidences. If Baker and Anderson had, like himself, been required to attend a meeting at short notice, then the operation he had carried out yesterday had stirred up a hornet's nest. Some-one was behind all this fuss, somebody vigorous and robust, quite unlike a run of the mill civil servant. It would not take long to verify that the orders were forgeries. The question was, how long would it take for them to react? Clearly, he would have to remove himself from the scene as quickly as possible. But, whether to go back to his apartment to collect other incriminating evidence? He might just have time.

Interrogation of Sergeant Baker and Captain Anderson

"And this was about 4 o'clock?"

"Yes Sir. I logged the orders in the normal way".

"And when you left Lieutenant Courtney here you didn't think it unusual to be sent back without him?"

"No, Sir. It is often the case that officers stay overnight, and, as a driver, I have to get back to my base as soon as possible".

"Very well, Sergeant. Thank you. That is all".
Sir Charles turned to his right and looked at the officer sitting next to him. "Well. What do you think?"

"Pretty straightforward, Charles. There's nothing amiss there". Sir Charles pondered for a moment, then pressed the intercom button.

"Captain Anderson please". After a moment, Anderson entered the room.

"Captain, I am Colonel Sir Charles Crayne. I'd like to ask you a few questions about yesterday. You telephoned Holmbury Commando base and asked Lieutenant Courtney to attend a meeting here as soon as possible. And you arranged for transport to pick him up immediately. Is that correct?"

"Yes Sir".

"Where did the orders originate?"

"They were a priority order issued by the Joint Chiefs, and delivered to Mr. Wright by hand, Sir".

"Were the instructions in proper order?"

"Yes, Sir. Duly stamped and signed".

"Do you know what the meeting was about?"

"No, Sir. Only that it was highly urgent."

"And after the meeting, what happened?"

"I was instructed to drive the Lieutenant to Ashdown Air Force base and leave him there, and then go off duty".

"Who gave you those instructions?"

"Mr. Wright".

"Do you know Mr. Wright well?"

"Not personally, Sir. But he had an appropriate security pass".

Sir Charles sat back in his chair. This was getting nowhere. "Thank you, Captain. That will be all." The Captain saluted and left.

Sir Charles spoke into the intercom. "Send in Mr. Wright, please".

"I have to say, Charles, there doesn't seem to be anything wrong, provided the orders are verified". It was the other officer speaking.

"That's certainly how it seems". Then, into the intercom, he repeated his previous request.   "Send in Mr. Wright please".

"He's a young man, this Courtney. Probably having a few days away with one of the clerks. He'll turn up". How Sir Charles wished that this were the case, in spite of the implications for Charlotte suggested in this version of possible events.

Sir Charles picked up the phone and called the secretary. After a few words with her he phoned reception security, to be told that Mr. Wright had left the building fifteen minutes ago to pick up a newspaper. The security man expressed surprise that he had not yet returned. Sir Charles phoned the police and asked them to go to Wright's address and detain him. Turning to his colleague Sir Charles uttered the words, "I think we have our man."

17.15 hours

It was too late. From his position at the corner of the street he could see two police cars. He saw a policeman leave the house carrying his briefcase, containing all the rubber stamps and other incriminating evidence. There was enough there to hang him. They had moved very fast, on this occasion, very unusual for the British. So, his spying career was, indeed, over. Now, he had to go to a safe house and lay low for a few weeks to assess the situation with his field controller. Wright could only hope that his involvement had helped the greater struggle.

18.15 hours

Sir Charles sat back in his chair, sipping coffee. Scores of people had arrived in the last thirty minutes and the War Office had become a hive of activity. As soon as the police searched Wright's apartment, and found the documents and equipment, the panic had started. Now, they had to discover how much damage had been caused, how much was ongoing, and how they could prevent any further damage. Sir Charles wondered bitterly how much of this activity was designed to cover up inefficiencies and complacency in the Department. He took no pleasure in being proved right, for it meant the worst possible outcome for James. He would now leave the matter in the hands of the police and military intelligence. They had promised to submit to him a preliminary report in a few days, with special reference to the incident concerning his missing officer. A full report would follow, 'in due course'.

As he left the War Office for the drive to Bishop's Lodge, he wondered what he would tell Charlotte.

Chapter 17

06.00 hours 31st August Northern France

Pierre Revol was 42 years old. His bad leg had kept him out of military service during France's short-lived war effort in 1939-40. He had continued, as before the War, to run his small bakery, and he had survived the hostilities thus far in reasonable condition.

In 1940 a German officer had been billeted in Revol's home, and the Frenchman lost no time in making it clear that the officer could expect to enjoy all home comforts. To Revol the shaming and abuse of his wife counted as nothing when set against the small concessions he had received from the military in return. He was able to smile, in all circumstances, at the invaders and occupiers of his country, and it was not a smile which concealed secret rage against a more powerful adversary, for, to Pierre Revol, the matter of most concern, the main priority, the paramount objective, was the prosperous survival of himself. The protection which any woman should expect from her husband had been completely absent. Mme. Revol had been forced to endure the worst which a defeated nation can expect from a brutal, victorious enemy; her debasement and degradation echoed the age-old experience of defenseless women confronted by the savage and barbarous soldiers of an invading army. In 1939 she had been a beautiful and admired woman; by 1944 she had become a slattern who had lost that most important of notions, self-respect. Now, she shunned the company of her neighbors. Her lack of communication meant that the blame for her situation could not be laid at the door of the real culprit, Pierre Revol.

As in his relationship with his wife, Revol would betray anyone or anything if it served his purpose. When the USA entered the war, bringing with it the distinct possibility of eventual Allied victory, he had joined the Resistance to ensure his position in the event of a German defeat. He had murdered a German soldier, the only course of action which earned genuine credibility amongst his compatriots, but he continued to inform the German authorities whenever he thought it safe and prudent to do so.

Now, this had happened. He had been asked to allow an Englishman, an agent of SOE, no less, to accompany him on his delivery route near Calais. The request had come from the British authorities, via the Resistance, and the request had specified him, by name, as the right man to help in the operation. No reason had been given for this choice by the British. In truth, Wright was merely passing on the orders as received from the SS. He had not been informed of the purpose or the nature of the operation. Minutes after he had received these instructions, Revol had informed his SS masters only to be told that he should carry out the request to the letter.

At 6am the agent arrived at Revol's bakery. He recognized him from previous missions. He could have warned him that the SS knew of his presence, but, why should he? Soon, the Allies would arrive, and the

Germans would be gone. Until then, this was certainly not the moment to declare war on the occupiers. No, the agent was walking into a trap, but these were the fortunes of war. C'est la vie.

They mounted the already loaded cart, and James asked Revol to go on his normal route. After an hour he asked him to stop. They had reached an area which was enclosed with barbed wire and mesh fencing. It looked to Revol like a derelict site, but what surprised him was the elaborate, but, even to his untrained eye, imperfect camouflage. James was also puzzled. There was nothing here, absolutely nothing suspicious, only a cordoned off area with makeshift camouflage. Odd, to say the least.

Odd, that is, unless it was intended to look suspicious from the air. The slightest frisson of unease shot along his spine. He returned to the cart and resumed his seat. He decided his best option was to just complete the round and then report back. He hoped one of the other agents sent in to the area had found more than he had. He wondered if Simon would have anything to do with the bombing; wondered if Sir Charles would be planning the Commando operation, wherever these operations were destined to be carried out.

As they came to a bend in the road they saw, a hundred yards ahead, a roadblock with a German Army truck. Several SS troops were lounging around. Revol turned to James. "What shall I do?"

"Carry on. There is no reason not to."

Revol wondered what the agent would do. Presumably, he would pretend to be a local; he probably had convincing papers. But the SS knew; they knew who he was. He was doomed; there was no possibility of escape. He amused himself with the idea of warning the agent, of giving him at least a fighting chance. Some hope!

At the roadblock the SS officer ordered them to dismount and accompany him to his office. Naturally, they complied with the instruction. The office was about fifty yards from the roadblock. James was completely calm. The officer sat down and addressed James. "Good morning, Hotel".
James felt a shiver run down his spine. "My name is..."

"Your name is James Courtney".

It was not a question. The officer knew; he was absolutely certain. James realized that there was no use in lying or blustering. He had to assess the situation quickly. Unaware of the role played by his Resistance companion, he felt he must absolve Revol of all complicity. That way the Resistance could be informed and, hopefully, mount an ambush. James spoke in English. He indicated Revol. "This man is completely unaware of my identity. He believes I am the cousin of a friend of his".

The officer smiled. He spoke to Revol. "You may go".

James was dismayed at this. It had been too easy. Something was not right here. Revol offered his cringing thanks and turned around. On his walk back to the cart he felt uneasy, as if all eyes were on him. He heard the sharp metallic crack of a rifle being cocked, made ready for use. A rifle? Surely, if they were going to shoot the Englishman, a pistol would be more appropriate. But why would they shoot him? There may be information to be gained here. Also, a rifle was for longer distances, not point-blank range, as in the case of the Englishman. There was no target at longer range. No target for a rifle. No such target, except himself. But that was foolish. He had always played fair with the Germans, given them help, information, his wife. They could not have anything against him. True, he had killed a German soldier, but they could not know that. No; in a few seconds the Englishman would be dead, and all Revol would have to do is explain his own escape. He would say that they had been stopped, and the Englishman had made a run for it. Of course, he had been caught and shot, whilst he, Revol, following severe questioning, and due to his good character during the occupation, had been released. They were not going to shoot him; it was the Englishman; it must be. God would protect him. God knew he had always done the right thing. The cart was a few yards away. Safety.

'Safety' was the last hope of his life, the final word in his mind as the bullet entered his body and shattered his spine. He died within moments, silently cursing all who survived.

"You need feel no sorrow for him". The SS officer was addressing James as he tied his hands behind his back. "He has betrayed everyone he knows. The world is a better place without him. Save your pity for yourself"

James was bundled into the waiting truck. The officer sat in the cab, with the driver, whilst three SS troops accompanied the prisoner. James was forced to lie face down, one of the German's boots resting firmly on his head.

07.30. Bishops Lodge

Charlotte woke at the normal time. She was in somber mood, putting this down to the normal process of waking. After a shower and break-fast she would be her normal, happy self. As usual, it would be a busy day at the hospital, so she would have no time for brooding, no time for introspection.

By midday her mood had not lifted. She was unable to concentrate properly on her duties. Luckily, important as these were, they were routine, so that her lack of concentration did not put any of the patients at risk. She would phone James as soon as she got home from the hospital. That would cheer her up.

Germany

The truck came to a halt. It had been a journey of several hours. Noting the heat and the position of the sun, James guessed it must be just after midday. They had travelled much faster in the last hour, and there had been fewer bumps in the road. So, the roads were better. They must have covered two hundred miles, possibly more. His body was numb from the enforced immobility. But his mind was as sharp as ever, and he believed they must be in Germany.

The officer came to the rear of the truck and lowered the tailgate. The prisoner was thrown onto a cobbled street and the soldiers jumped down after him. Everywhere he looked James could see bombed out buildings, offices, shops and residential premises. War was a costly affair. They were in a semi-rural environment, on the outskirts, perhaps, of a big city. Hamburg? Hannover? Perhaps Cologne, which was less distant from where he had been captured than was Hamburg, but maybe they were trying to mislead him. As he was a British serviceman out of uniform, he could expect to be shot as a spy. He wondered if Charlotte was aware of his predicament. He cursed himself bitterly for putting her through another ordeal, especially after promising himself that he would avoid this at all costs.

James was seized by the arms and dragged roughly down the steps of a cellar. He was pushed through a stout door beyond which lay a passage leading deeper. Some distance along the passage they came to a second door. The officer led James through the door and down more steps into a dingy room with a concrete floor. In the center was a table with a chair on either side. Above the table burned a single light bulb. There was a bunk by the far wall. Against the longest wall a substantial wooden post had been fixed, with metal hooks along each side. There were further hooks concreted into the wall in roughly vertical but irregular lines. Opposite the door was a wall with a short, fixed bench. On top of the bench was a wooden frame construction. The two vertical sides had holes cut in them, and were joined across the front by a wide plank with a hole cut into-it. The whole construction resembled the public stocks in which offenders used to be imprisoned in such a way that passers-by could throw rotting fruit and other matter at them. There was sawdust on the floor beneath the frame. The whole room looked ominously like a torture chamber. The officer took James' shoes off and tied him to one of the chairs, which proved to be fixed to the floor. Without a word he left the room and bolted the door from the outside.

As his eyes became accustomed to the dimness, James glimpsed a basin in a corner, with a dripping tap. There was a broken mirror fixed to the wall and a light bulb above. Presumably this was so that prisoners' morale could be destroyed as they saw their facial features damaged by the brutality of the torture. He heard the sound of rats or mice scurrying somewhere nearby. The room was dank, airless and windowless; the chance of escape, nil.

After a while he heard the sound of footsteps from outside the door. The bolt was drawn back and the door opened. Someone entered the room and closed the door behind him. James could see, in the arc of light thrown by the light bulb, the leather boots of a German officer. As the stranger descended the steps his uniform came into view. It was a senior SS officer. His face still concealed by the dark, he approached the table and put down a briefcase. For a moment he surveyed the scene before him, allowing his eyes to become accustomed to the dimness, and then sat down. James looked directly into the leering, gloating face of Sturmbannfuehrer Otto Stockhausen.

"Hotel, at last we meet, but now, under conditions of my choosing". He paused for a moment. "As Mark Twain might say, reports of my death were greatly exaggerated".

James recovered quickly from the shock. "I presume you wish to know the purpose of my mission?" He would have to hold out for twenty-four hours. This was the period of time, it was believed, which would give others in his organization the opportunity to take appropriate action, on the understanding that 99% of prisoners would succumb under torture and answer any question to end the pain. He hoped the launch site for the new missile had been identified and bombed by now. It may be of some value if he could convince Stockhausen that bombing would be the Allies' only response. If he could conceal the intended use of Commandos, this would give them a better chance.

"No. I'm not interested. But do tell me this. When you landed last night at about 22.30, you made your way to a small farm and spent the night with a woman. Did you stay there on all your missions?"

Silently, James cursed Revol for his treachery. "I stayed last night at Revol's bakery".

"Stein". It was a call to someone outside the room. "Bring in the woman".

The door was flung open and an SS trooper dragged a struggling, blond-haired woman down the steps. He forced her to kneel at the table, and then left the room. James recognized Sophie, his hostess from the previous night.

"You stayed last night with her". Stockhausen was not asking a question. It was a statement.

"I've never seen her before".

"Well, in that case, you won't mind if I enjoy her womanly charms".

James said nothing, but Sophie spoke. "I'd rather die first".

Stockhausen looked at the woman. "You'd rather die first?" He looked at James. "She'd rather die first". He leapt from his chair, drawing his pistol. He pulled her hair back and held the barrel against her left eye. "And so you shall, my pretty. So you shall".

There was silence, punctuated only by the rapid breathing of Sophie. James could hear his heart pounding. After an endless minute, Stockhausen let go of her hair and sat down, laughing. A wave of relief swept over both prisoners. Abruptly, Stockhausen raised the gun and fired a single bullet into Sophie's left eye. The back of her head seemed to disintegrate as she was thrown across the room. The door opened and Stein rushed in. "Take this mess away". The soldier carried out his orders without a word.

Stockhausen continued "Your friend and accomplice, Artis, recently of the magnificent French Resistance, died in much the same way. He was captured, unconscious, at St Michel bay, following your..unsuccessful? ...raid on Foin. He was taken to a cell which contained a clock. He was revived by a 'doctor' and told that he had been unconscious for ten hours. When questioned, he revealed that you were to be picked up at St. Michel bay at midnight and would, by now, be back in England. The clock was set six hours fast. I put it right and ordered a squad of my men to St Michel immediately. You escaped, as we know, by seconds. But Artis died believing that his foolishness had betrayed you. It was such fun".

James was horrified by the murder of Sophie, and by the story of Artis. He vowed, silently, to kill Stockhausen.

"As for your mission to discover the launch site of our new bombs, it was doomed to failure from the start. There is no site. They are on mobile launchers. At this moment they are being driven to points in German occupied Belgium. In less than 24 hours London will be a devastated city. Blast, heat and radiation will devastate all life in a ten-mile radius. If the wind happens to be in the right direction, poisonous gases will be blown as far as....Bishop's Lodge, so that your dear friends, Sir Charles and his daughter, and your brother, if he is there, will suffer a slow, painful, choking death.

It was time for James to speak. "In a few months, there will be four million Allied troops, with plenty of supplies, attacking Germany from the west, as well as four million Russians attacking from the east. Even if London is obliterated, Germany is finished. Nazism will be swept away. What will happen to you then?"

"What do you mean?"

"If you release me and tell me where the missiles are now, I guarantee to take you to England as a regular army prisoner. After the war, you will be released back into civilian life. That is not the fate which awaits most of the SS". It was the only card James had to play.

For a moment, Stockhausen seemed to consider the offer, then he laughed. "Once London is incinerated the Allies will be given 12 hours to agree to terms. There are atomic devices concealed in seven American cities, plus bombs intended for use against the sub-humans from the East. They will certainly agree to a ceasefire. This war will be over much sooner than you think, and with an outcome far from what you expected when you embarked on this mad adventure. The Americans will be sent home and we will occupy England. I shall take as my HQ..." he pondered for a moment. "...Bishop's Lodge, and, if she is, somehow, still alive, I will take Charlotte as my...companion? As for the Russians, we will bomb then into oblivion in any case".

James could see some clear contradictions in this story. The bomb which Stockhausen mentioned would damage Bishop's Lodge, so why would he expect to take it as his headquarters? As for the revolting threat to Charlotte, this was clearly meant to destroy James' morale. In fact, all of this was completely untrue. Germany was months away from developing an atomic bomb, and Stockhausen's real intention was to leave Germany in a few days by a well-established SS escape route and start a new, opulent and safe life in Canada. All of this fantasy was psychological torment for the prisoner, revenge for countless humiliations, which was the prelude to the physical torture he intended to carry out personally.

"As for your future, Hotel, you may be surprised to learn that I do not intend to kill you. On the contrary, I intend to release you in about 24 hours". James knew that there must be more to this than Stockhausen had said. He continued. "When you leave here, you will be a free man". Stockhausen stood up and took his briefcase. He walked up the steps and opened the door. With a final leer at James, he left the room.

Wedel A small town 30 miles from Hamburg, location of the dungeon

James had been alone for hours. He felt the rising tide of panic, the worst enemy of an agent, welling up in his mind. He must keep control of himself. He must assume that Stockhausen's story was untrue. He must keep calm. Yet, the time spent alone in this dungeon had given his imagination all the time it needed to invent the most dreadful specters. He breathed deeply, forced himself to focus. Think only of escape. Whatever his situation, he was still a serving British officer, and it was his duty, as well as his inclination, to strain every sinew and muscle to act against the enemy. He tried to rock the chair; it was fixed too firmly. He tried to free his hands; the rope cut sharply into his flesh. Adrenalin poured into his bloodstream; his muscles burned with the effort. All to no avail. Finally, exhausted, he fell into an uneasy sleep.

6am Friday 1st September. Bishops Lodge

Charlotte had not slept all night. The depression of the previous day had deepened.
She had not been able to speak to James; 'summoned to London' was all the orderly could tell her. In the 12 hours since she had phoned Holmbury her depression had become doubts, and her doubts, fear. The message she had left asked James to phone her as soon as he returned, whatever the time. She had repeated and stressed the last phrase to impress it on the orderly's mind. There had been no phone call. Maybe the orderly had gone off duty and forgotten to pass on the message, a thought that did not reassure Charlotte.
Unable to sleep, and uncomfortable in bed, she had come downstairs several hours earlier. She now sat at the table in the kitchen, looking, by candlelight, at the photograph of James which she had brought downstairs. Her thoughts terrified her, for however much she tried to imagine their future together, she could only remember the fearful past, only the bad times. She felt he was receding, slipping away, creating, against both their wills, a gulf, unbridgeable in time or space. The fear was unbearable.
She was vaguely aware of a rattling sound in the kitchen, a key in a lock. Somewhere, a door open and closed. She heard someone call her name softly. It was a woman's voice, familiar and kindly. The voice continued softly, inaudibly, as a robe was wrapped around her, covering her semi-nakedness. Then the voice was gone. Alone once more. Alone with her thoughts. With her fears.

6am Friday 1st September Wedel

A sound interrupted his dozing. The bolts were drawn back and the door opened slowly. A young girl entered the dungeon. She could not have been older than fourteen. She was dressed in the uniform of the Hitler Youth; a white blouse, a short, black skirt, white ankle socks and white canvas shoes. In one hand she held a pistol, in the other, a dagger. She walked slowly to where James was tied up and carefully, she cut the ropes binding his hands. By the time he had released his feet she had left the room and bolted the door again.

It would take a few minutes for the circulation to get back to normal, a process which he assisted by vigorous massage of his wrists and ankles. His mind worked rapidly. He tried to weigh the pros and cons of each possible course of action which might become available to him. He had to believe that England was still at war, and so, therefore, was he. Everything that he loved and cherished may be in imminent danger, but he could achieve nothing without escape. The possibility of making a deal with Stockhausen was negligible. Obviously, there was a deep vendetta, and, in any case, he believed that the German was quite insane. No reasonable responses could be expected. But the other SS men may be more amenable to threats or bribery. For this course of action to succeed, Stockhausen would have to be removed from the scene, preferably by his death, preferably at James' hands.

James resolved to wait until they were alone and then attack. He looked around for a weapon. There was none to be found. In his exhausted state, he could not be sure of overcoming Stockhausen in unarmed combat, especially as he could summon help with just a shout. He would have to choose the moment carefully. He would seize Stockhausen's own weapon and turn it against him. If the remaining SS troops acted hastily and shot him, well, that was probably no worse than Stockhausen's real plans for him. He decided to lay on the bunk and get as much rest as possible.

James barely had time to close his eyes before he heard the sound of approaching boots. He reached the chair just as the door bolts were drawn back. Stein entered the dungeon, accompanied by two fellow SS thugs. The three of them walked slowly down the steps, whilst the young girl sat on the top step, still carrying the pistol. The door remained slightly ajar, allowing some light from outside partially to illuminate the darker recesses of the prison.

"Stand up, Hotel". Stein's voice was harsh and threatening. His stance and bearing were, like his cronies, aggressive. James was certain he was about to endure a beating.

"What's your name?" James called to the girl.

"Gisela".

The three men now stood at the bottom of the stairs, barring the only escape route with their massive frames. Slowly, they started to walk the few paces towards James, but stopped when he suddenly leapt up and stepped to the other side of the table.

"Gisela, give me the gun". James had to try even the remotest possibility, if he were to survive the next few hours. Children, he knew, could be unpredictable. Gisela certainly was. She threw the gun to him. His heart leaped as he caught the weapon and pointed it at his adversaries, who now stood quite still. Fixing Stein with a direct gaze,

James spoke. "I can guarantee that you will be treated fairly, according to the Geneva Convention, and that I personally will ensure you are treated as prisoners of war, and not as war criminals. In return, you will lead me to a safe place and give me the information I require". James hand and voice trembled with exhaustion and expectation.

Stein laughed. Without a word, the three started, again, to walk towards James.

Clearly, they would not make any deal. There was no other course open to him; he would have to shoot his way out. If it happened that there were several more SS outside the building, well, at least his death would be quick and relatively painless. He backed away, hoping that even in these last few seconds the trio might reconsider. Finally, his back came up against the wall.

"This is your last chance". Stein was now about two yards away. James raised the gun to point it directly at Stein's eyes, and yet, in some suicidal gesture, the man continued advancing. James pressed the trigger. The gun clicked. He pressed the trigger again; again, it clicked, and again, and a fourth time. The gun was not loaded. Peals of girlish laughter filled the room, echoing around and around. James had demonstrated that he was prepared to kill Stein. He could only expect that Stein would take account of this. He knew now that he had no possibility of avoiding death.

Bishops Lodge.

"Sir Charles. Sir Charles". Cooks voice was urgent and agitated, sufficiently so to wake the man. He had arrived home in the early hours after a long and depressing day and had left a note that he should not be disturbed until 10am. It was now just after 8. Before he had time to protest, cook continued. "Sir Charles, it's Miss Charlotte. She's sitting downstairs just staring straight ahead. She has a terrible look on her face. There's something wrong".

Sir Charles did not need what he thought was this woman's twaddle at this time of day, but then they both heard the unmistakable sound of Charlotte's voice from downstairs, and it required an immediate response. She had screamed.

Wedel

Stein's cronies each grasped one of James arms and, bending the fingers back, pinned him to the wall. Stein kicked James viciously in the testicles. His legs buckled as he let out a low groan, but, supported on both sides, was unable to fall to the ground. Stein dragged him upright by the hair and smashed his fist into his abdomen, just below the ribs. James gasped for breath, as Stein stamped his boot down hard on James' left foot. He howled in pain as Stein delivered three thundering kicks in quick succession to James' right shin. Unsupported now, he fell to the ground, turning his back towards his oppressors. Stein now sent a crippling kick into James kidneys. From somewhere James could hear laughter. Then he heard Stein's voice.

"Gisela". The laughter stopped, and James was aware of small footsteps on the concrete. He heard the tap being turned on, and a vessel being filled. He felt a cold blast as water was thrown into his face. Nearer now, the laughter started again, the sickeningly depraved sound of a perverse child. They pulled James to his feet. Stein pushed him against the wall and approached menacingly.

Bishops' Lodge

She screamed again. He had never seen her like this. He embraced her; tried to comfort and console her, tried to control her dangerously flouncing contortions. Again, she screamed, a tortured, demented roar. The tension in her body transmitted itself to him. This was no ordinary nightmare. This was something inhumanly real and gruesome.

"Phone Dr. Young. Tell him to come at once. For God's sake, hurry". Sir Charles' voice trembled as he spat out the words. Cook did not need to be told a second time.

Wedel

Summoning up the last vestiges of his strength and courage, having decided that these were the last moments of his life, James smashed his fist into Stein's face. His nose exploded like a tomato. He staggered back and fell to the floor. Slowly, he got to his feet.

"I have to say that I admire you for that. In your hopeless position, given that the remainder of your life will be short and painful, I think I would have done the same. And I'm sure I would have found, as you are about to discover, that the reprisals were not worth the fleeting moment of pleasure. Goodbye, Hotel". Without another word, all three set upon James. Blows rained down on every part of his body. Twice, he was revived with water, to endure more punishment.

Finally, it ceased. James body was battered and bruised, but he felt, strangely, that they had deliberately avoided his face, and also that there were no broken bones. He heard them leaving the room, and

Stein's last words. "Come, Gisela. I'm ready for you now". Mercifully, James lost consciousness.

Bishops' Lodge.

After what seemed, to Sir Charles, a lifetime of struggling with his daughter, she was, at last, peaceful. It was an eerie, haunted calm, the atmosphere taut with dangerous potential. The doctor had arrived just after the trauma had finished, so that he had not witnessed the worst excesses. His diagnosis had to be based on the account of Sir Charles and cook, themselves seemingly agitated beyond any normal state. True, her pulse was rather faster than it should be, so he knew that something had happened. But, a nightmare, very realistic, very frightening, *must* be the cause of all this upset. A mild tranquillizer would do the trick. That, and a good, long, deep sleep was all that she would need. And, yes, he did have time for a cup of tea.

08.00hours Wedel

It seemed no time at all before Stein and his men returned. James felt himself being lifted onto the bench. His arms and legs were secured with rope, and his head was placed in the stocks he had noticed earlier. The frame was adjusted and fixed into position. The vertical beams were pressed against the sides of his head and secured. A bucket of cold water quickly brought him to an unwelcome consciousness. His head was completely immobile; he had no significant movement in any part of his body. He was completely defenseless. He was terrified.
"Well, Hotel. This is where we say goodbye. But you won't be alone for long.
Stockhausen will be along very soon to pay his respects". Stein and his men departed. James was completely alone, wondering what the next few hours had in store. All he could see were the thing directly ahead of him, the table and the other chair. He could hear the tap dripping.
After a few minutes he heard the sound of footsteps approaching. It was Stockhausen. He walked up to the table and placed a tattered briefcase on top. James noticed that he had exchanged his uniform for civilian clothes that had obviously seen better days. In fact, he looked almost like a refugee. He opened the briefcase and took out a length of rubber tube with a hollow glass hook attached to one end. There was also an ordinary, metal kitchen skewer, adapted to make a barb at the end, a cigar, and a small glass jar with a screw top. Out of his pocket he took a small piece of wood and a chisel. Without speaking, he took the plain end of the rubber tube and attached it to the tap. He took the end

with the hook and satisfied himself that it reached the table. He turned on the water.

"Hotel. It is clear that you have carried out murder and other crimes against the German nation in our struggle for our justified and legitimate ambitions. I must now pass and execute sentence upon you. I have decided to spare your life, but I must ensure that you are not in a position to carry out further acts of aggression against us. I have decided to deprive you of the powers of speech, sight and hearing. Have you anything to say?"

Bishops Lodge

It was time for the doctor to leave. Sir Charles stood by the front door as the doctor went to check that all was well with Charlotte, who should be in a deep sleep by now. He looked at the clear blue sky, breathed deeply of the fresh, clean country air, briefly inspected the doctor's car, passing the moments. But, so many moments.

"Doctor?" A gentle inquiry. There was no reply. He walked into the hall, from where he would be able to see into the room where they had left Charlotte. He could see the doctor in the doorway. He seemed transfixed by something in the room. Sir Charles joined him. They stood together, mortified by the apparition before them. Charlotte was dragging her fingernails down her cheeks, causing deep welts from which blood began to ooze. Her eyes were wild and bulging, her mouth open with her lips pulled back exposing her teeth. The veins in her head and neck were visibly pulsating. It was as if she were screaming silently.

This situation did not last long. Suddenly, she emitted an ear-piercing bellow. Sir Charles rushed to her and embraced her, trying to give her comfort, security. The doctor was already loading a hypodermic syringe. Again, she screamed. And again.

Wedel

James shuddered as a wave of horror swept over him. Speechless with fear, he stared at his captor. Stockhausen's eyes were glaring, almost luminous with some inhuman power, his lips trembled. He was certainly insane, and quite capable of carrying out his threats. Now, terrified, James was unable to respond, unable to think, aware only of the pounding of his heart. Please Charlotte. Now Charlotte. If you can do it, do it now. His thoughts raced. He was moments from the destruction of his senses, of all that made life good and wholesome. He prayed. He begged God for escape. He begged Charlotte to rescue him. Or Sir Charles. Or Simon. He watched Stockhausen take a spatula, load it with caustic substance from the jar, approach him. He closed his eyes and mouth, but Stockhausen prized open his jaws with the chisel, inserting the wooden block to prevent James from closing his mouth. James could not spit out the wood, could barely breathe.

Grinning inanely, Stockhausen displayed the acidic compound before James' eyes. He pressed his body against his defenseless victim and plunged the spatula into his mouth, smearing his tongue with the acrid substance. The bitter taste was immediately obvious, but the warmth was almost comforting. For a moment James felt a frisson of hope, as if Stockhausen had only been bluffing, perhaps there was going to be an interrogation after all. Then, as if some barrier had suddenly failed, excruciating pain scorched through his mouth and throat. James body arched as he screamed and gagged. He could smell the burning of his own flesh, could hear the hiss as the chemical destroyed his tongue. Outraged and agonized, James screamed again and again. Stockhausen suddenly withdrew the spatula and inserted the glass hook. Cold water poured into James' mouth, cooling, cleansing, rinsing away the burning acid. James gagged again, spluttering, expelling the toxic mixture of acid and water. If Stockhausen had delayed any longer, James might have swallowed the substance and died. That was not the plan at all. That would be a premature death.

The coldness of the water brought some temporary relief from the burning but did nothing to ease the strained muscles and sinews of his neck and throat. Through his pain James was able to grasp that his tongue had been destroyed. Never again would he be able to form words properly. He was sickened by the intimacy of this violation, petrified at the thought of the ravages his captor might perpetrate against him.

Bishops Lodge

The dose of tranquillizer had worked for a few moments, but then the trauma had started again. "For God's sake, give her some more". Sir Charles' plea was the understandable demand of a parent caught up in the unimaginable trauma of his child.

"I can't. I daren't. She's already had enough to knock out a horse". The doctor was almost in despair. They struggled to control her, to prevent her from injuring herself. Her strength was awesome. Again, she screamed and choked, her face distorted horribly. Was there no end to this nightmare?

Wedel

For several minutes Stockhausen left the tube in James' mouth. He wanted to ease the pain, to let him recover so that the next punishment would be all the more effective. He removed the tube and held the skewer so that James could see it. He held the instrument horizontally and jerked it forward. He twisted it, and then pulled it back, revealing to James what his next punishment would be. He inserted his finger into his victim's ear. James was filled with revulsion and nausea that this depraved man should penetrate his body.

Stockhausen pushed the skewer through the hole in the vertical beam and rammed it deep into James' left ear. A screech of agony was accompanied by a tensing of all the muscles in his head, neck and throat. The skewer was withdrawn and held in front of James eyes. Attached to the barb was some blood and a small amount of tissue. He placed his finger in the right ear, a revolting act which James endured in relative silence. James roared as the skewer followed.

Bishops Lodge

Her eyes were bloodshot Her breathing was fast and shallow. She was drenched in sweat. Like a mortally wounded dog, she emitted a low, guttural growl. She held her head in her hands, her body shaking. They stood, bewildered, as she looked upwards and bellowed in pain and rage, inhumanly loud and long. Again, Sir Charles embraced her, a useless gesture, completely unequal to the situation, done for his own sake, as the doctor looked on in stunned impotence.

Wedel

Stockhausen crouched so that his eyes were at the same level as James'. Smiling, he placed the lighted cigar between his lips and sucked. He felt the comforting smoke enter his lungs, and, more important, saw the tip glow. Even more important than this, he knew that James also could see the incandescent tip. Even in his traumatized state James resolved a final act of defiance. He would not close his eyes, a futile effort, in any case, and deprive the madman of the chance to use his force. The monster continued to suck the cigar, watching James' face for signs of fear, savoring the moment, glad that he had left this particular procedure to the end.
Surely, he thought, loss of sight must be the worst fate to befall a young, fit person. One final suck left the cigar half used. Time was getting on; there had been plenty of physical as well as psychological torture. He took the cigar from his mouth and held it a few inches from James face. At the last moment James' courage failed. He shut his eyes and tried to

move his head to the side. Useless and futile. Stockhausen easily prized open his eyes. In quick succession Stockhausen stubbed the glowing tip into each eye. James emitted a strangled groan as the pain registered in his brain. This was the final straw. With divine mercy, the brain caused the entire body to become numb and closed down its own responses. James fell into unconsciousness.

Stockhausen untied the ropes binding his victim. He loosened and removed the beams and stocks. James' flaccid body fell to the ground. Satisfied with his days' work Stockhausen joined his waiting driver who had instructions to take him to a little-known airfield nearby, where Stockhausen was to board a plane to Southern Germany, conveniently close to the Swiss border. A few days here, and then a further trip to Spain, and finally, a plane to Canada, as a displaced person with relatives in Ottawa.

Bishops Lodge

Her vomit dripped from Sir Charles' face, down his neck and onto the floor. He was unaware of this. It had been her final paroxysm. She was now unconscious. Cook and the doctor stood by as Sir Charles carried her upstairs to her bedroom. Tenderly, he laid her on a large towel on the floor and fetched a bowl of warm water. Tearfully, he stripped her and washed her body. He dried her and lifted her gently onto the bed. After covering her with a sheet and a few blankets, he kissed her. Then, the doctor entered the room. After a brief examination, he assured Sir Charles that she was asleep. She would now sleep for several hours, with regular checks by cook or Sir Charles. They went downstairs without exchanging a single word. Inevitably, cook was making a pot of strong tea. Sir Charles welcomed the normality, but many questions haunted him. Above all, the question which obsessed him, the question which caused an unaccustomed fear throughout his being, now occupied his thoughts. How bad were things for James?

Wedel, Germany

Slowly, he drifted back into a pitiful awareness. He was on a hard floor, intensely cold, and yet every part of his body burned with agony. He could only breathe in shallow gulps. Every movement caused pain to shoot through his tortured body. Whimpering in solitary distress he got shakily to his feet, using the wall as support. It was pitch black and unnaturally silent. He wondered if he were dead! Slowly, trying to gather his wits, trying to make sense of his situation, he moved along the wall until he came to the corner. He continued feeling his way along the adjacent wall until he bumped into an obstacle, which he soon identified as the sink. Locating the tap, he turned it on. The water gushed over his hands. He rinsed his hands and face and drank deeply of the refreshing liquid.

Suddenly, he stopped. For long minutes he stood motionless, his mind ponderously collecting information, trying to remember what had happened. He knelt down next to the sink, one hand under the flowing water, the other to his forehead. With an anguished cry he realized that he could not hear the splash.

Gradually, his sobbing subsided. He decided to get out of the room and take stock of his situation. With his hand outstretches he moved gingerly forward. He touched something, and quickly withdrew his hand as he felt a burning sensation. Cautiously, he moved his hand forward until he established the location of the hot object. He covered his hand with his shirt sleeve and gently touched the object. It moved away, but then moved back. He took hold of it and held it, examined it, until the heat became too intense. It was the light bulb, and if it were hot, it was illuminated. And yet, it was pitch black; all was in darkness. The memory flooded back, and the rage, and the fear. James turned around and moved blindly, recklessly forward. He tripped over something and slumped onto the table. He banged the top of the table with his fists and raged against Stockhausen as the realization of his condition dawned on him again, and with it, returned the pain and the anguish and the fear.

He staggered over to where he knew the bunk was and collapsed onto it. His last thought before he fell asleep was of his beloved Charlotte. He dreamed about her, dressed in white, her beautiful, kind face smiling at him, her soft hands caressing him, stroking away all the pain and misery, her body, loving him, cocooning him, protecting him.

It was early September 1944. He was at an unknown location. He had no means of contacting anyone who would be friendly. He was physically, emotionally and mentally damaged beyond his imagination. He did not know where to turn. He could not speak, see or hear. This was the way he would have to spend the rest of his life. Mercifully, he fell into a disturbed sleep

09.00 hours 4th September

Sir Charles spread a thin veneer of butter on his toast and wondered idly how long rationing would last after the end of hostilities. He heard the sound of movement from upstairs. Charlotte must have got up. She had been silent and morose since the traumatic incidents of the previous Friday. Dr. Young had called in on Saturday and again on Sunday and had assured his friend that his daughter was in good physical condition. They had discussed what would be the best time, from a medical point of view, to break the news to her of James' capture by the Germans. The doctor had suggested that sooner was better than later. She could then start to come to terms with the situation, and although it would increase her pain, in the long run it would prove better to get over this hurdle as soon as possible. Sir Charles agreed.

Charlotte joined him but declined the offer of food. She took just a cup of tea. They sat for several minutes without speaking. Sir Charles was about to break the silence with some small talk when the phone rang. He hoped it was the call he had been waiting for all weekend from a friend in military intelligence. After the normal greetings Sir Charles listened for ten minutes without uttering a word. Finally, he said, "And what about the boy?" There was a brief, hesitant reply from the person at the other end of the phone, and then sir Charles thanked his friend and hung up.

With a heavy heart he went to his bedroom and spent an hour thinking about James. His mind ranged over the happy years they had spent together, when a bond of mutual trust, respect and admiration had formed between them. He thought of the post-war future, with James as his son-in-law, and, perhaps, a couple of grandchildren. This was now just an impossible dream, for there was practically no doubt about the course of events. James had certainly been lured into a trap by a civil servant traitor and had been taken by the Germans. Lieutenant James Courtney had died in the service of his country, and all that remained was a golden memory. He wept, unashamedly unable to control his emotions. He hoped there would be no repetition of this weakness when he told Charlotte, which he decided to do at once. He found her sitting at the dining table where he had left her earlier. She was staring at a photograph of James.

"Charlotte, I have to talk to you". He spoke softly, hesitantly. There was no reply. "Can you hear me?"

"Yes, Daddy". He was surprised at the firmness of her voice, as if she had been preparing herself for the coming revelations.

"Charlotte, for the last four years James has been involved in special duties". His words came slowly, were chosen carefully, for he had to admit to a degree of deviousness. "He's been on scores of missions behind enemy lines..."

"And you both told me about Coastal Command because you didn't want me to worry. That's fine". The words were almost whispered, spoken without accusation or recrimination. She continued to stare at the photograph.

"Yes. That was James' idea. Mostly he operated in the area around Calais, and he was extremely successful." She did not care where he had operated; did not care how successful he had been. These were things that mattered only to men. Nothing, no price, no overwhelming success could compensate her for the loss of the only man she had ever loved. She remained calm as her father continued.

"Unfortunately, the Germans discovered his identity, apparently from a sympathizer in the War Office, and he became a particular target for revenge, especially by one high ranking SS officer who seems to have had an implacable vendetta against him. They set a trap for him, and we are sure that he was captured last Thursday". He paused, fearful of her reaction. There was none. She continued to stare at the photograph, nodding her head as if she were receiving confirmation of something she already knew. "I received information this morning that the Resistance in the area was wiped out last Thursday night. It was sudden, unexpected and thorough. We don't know if James was in uniform or in civilian clothes, but either way, it is almost certain that he was captured, and almost certainly they will have taken their revenge". He could think of no other way to put it without using the word 'killed'

At the last word she stopped nodding her head. She turned her head and looking directly into her father's eyes she said. "James is not dead". She looked back at the photograph. "He is in terrible trouble. Terrible, terrible trouble. But he is definitely, *definitely,* alive" A single tear trickled from her eye. Her father was touched by her courage, and by the calmness of her manner. But he was gravely concerned for her future. For her to have any future, she must accept, be made to accept, that James was dead.

Wedel 4th September

He had no idea how long he had been there. He knew that the pain was beginning to subside, and that he had survived the initial trauma. Nobody had touched him for a long time, so he assumed that his tormentors had gone, but also that there was no-one in his immediate vicinity who would, or could, help him. His natural strength of mind and his will were beginning to reassert themselves after the crisis brought by the realization of his condition had passed. Reality was now clear to him; he was blind and deaf, and, judging by the scarring on his tongue and mouth, he would not be able to make meaningful, coherent sounds. Doubt and uncertainty surrounded his future, but in all this misery, there was one possibility he had to believe, one chance that he had to count on; Charlotte would come for him. She would know he was alive. She would receive the usual 'lost in action, presumed killed' telegram, and not accept it as the end of his story. He did not know how long it would take, but he was sure that, eventually, she would find him.

Unless, that is, Stockhausen's words had been true, and London had been devastated, the War, now, in its last hours. Perhaps they did not have an atomic bomb. Maybe it had just been a trap to ensnare him. He could not help but envisage all these possibilities, all these fears. He might never find out how the War ended; he might not live long enough, but it was crucial to believe, to hope and, above all, to survive. He must cling to the belief that the Allies would win the War and occupy Germany. Then, all displaced persons would be processed, and, whenever possible, returned to their homes. Stockhausen had not seemed to realize, when he tried to destroy James, that he could still write. But he would have to be careful; if he wrote in English, he might leave himself vulnerable to attack by the spiteful thugs who are present in all societies. For the moment, if he wrote anything, it would be in German.

The immediate problem was food. There would be shortages in Germany, just as in England. The population would be hard pressed. He could not hope to earn or steal enough to live on. Reluctantly, he had to accept that he must beg, and to do so successfully, he must get to a population center as soon as possible.

He found his way out of the dungeon. He knew that he was outside because he could feel the warmth of the sun and smell the freshness of the air. The clement weather was his first piece of luck. His second was to find, almost immediately, the small branch of a tree, which he would be able to strip of its bark and use as a stick. He did not know, and would not know for months, that he also had a third piece of luck. Having no information on which to make a decision, he chose to turn right. If he had been able to see, he would have recognized a signpost, pointing in the direction he had chosen, indicating the great city of Hamburg, and the chance of help. It showed the distance as 40 kilometers. It was destined to be a tortuous journey of more than one hundred days.

12th September.

However frustrating it may be, he had to persevere. There was no choice. He must continue his search until he found what he was looking for. The alternative was to spend more nights like the last two, when he had tried, with little success, to sleep in the cold, blustery conditions prevalent at this time of year. He had only a thin shirt, quite inadequate for protection against the elements. And this was early September; the prospects for November and December were not encouraging. He dared not think about January and February. This was why he would have to grovel through the ruins of buildings like this until he found warmer clothing, or a blanket. He had no idea if he were being scrutinized by the occupants, if any, of the building; no notion of whether he was regarded with the contempt usually reserved for those who rob graves, or corpses. But this is what he would have to do to survive. He was not even certain that there were people around. No-one had touched him since he had left the SS torture room a few days earlier. His world was one of complete isolation; quite black and totally silent.

His search had so far yielded what he thought were a small hand towel and a table cloth. Not sufficient for his needs, but it suggested he was in a domestic house, so there was the chance of finding clothing. Eventually, his groping hand touched the sleeve of a substantial coat. This would be ideal, but further investigation revealed a problem. The coat was on a corpse, not yet decomposing. For a few moments James hesitated, trying to assess the possibilities. The corpse was stone cold, dead for some time. The skull seemed to be caved in, perhaps the result of falling masonry. He soon decided that this was too good an opportunity to ignore. He would always be in ignorance of the presence of other people, and of their attitude to this theft from a dead man. He could only hope that common sense would prevail and that his own deprivation would explain and justify his actions. On this occasion, he was wrong. Most of the people near to him were preoccupied with their own calamities following the recent air attack to pay any attention to this beggarly figure rummaging through the debris of what had previously been a house. But, nearby, sat a youth, callow, brutalized by the War, who could not countenance this simple act of self-preservation. As James struggled to remove the garment from the corpse, the youth sent a well-aimed kick into his face, sending him sprawling, painfully, onto a mound of rubble. James lay perfectly still, anticipating a violent follow-up. None came. He groveled amongst the dust and bricks until he found his stick, and slowly, laboriously, hauled himself to his feet. With faltering steps he struggled back to the road, and away from this place where he had a dangerous enemy.

This act of brutality had been witnessed, and ignored, by several people, but one person watched, and resolved to help James. It was a little girl, ten years old, orphaned by the air-raid, the daughter of the corpse with the coat. Death and destruction had surrounded her, it seemed, for most of her life, and her simple belief was that James' action was exactly what her father would have wanted. She followed him until she was sure he was settled for the night. When he woke, he found himself covered with a thick coat. In one of the pockets was a small piece of bread.

It would be fourteen weeks before luck smiled on James sufficiently for him to find shelter and relative safety. This would happen, appropriately, on Christmas Day. In the meantime, there would be *several examples of the kindness shown by the little girl, but there were to be many more examples of the youth's hostility.*

"Come in, Sir Charles. Please, take a seat." The doctor indicated a chair with a wave of his hand. "I'll get straight to the point as we're both busy men. I've contacted a number of people who specialize in the field of emotional disturbance, and the opinion is unanimous. For her own sake, she must be made to accept that Lieutenant Courtney is dead. It is very common, indeed, normal, for people to believe that their loved one is still alive, but it's a feeling rooted in irrational disbelief, an inability to face the facts. In Charlotte's case it is complicated by the belief that she has, and which you, apparently share, that she <u>had</u> some sort of supernatural connection to James. Now, if this belief, which most of my colleagues do not share, is strong enough, it may continue to affect her judgement even beyond his passing. She's a young woman and, if I may say so, an attractive one. Her future happiness depends on her future social contacts, not on the memories of a lost love. If there is any substantial delay in her acceptance of the facts, her belief that he's alive will become so firmly fixed in her mind that she may wait in hope for years. Perhaps, forever." The slow, deliberate delivery of this last word was not lost on Sir Charles. "So, the process of convincing her cannot start too soon. Remember, after she has accepted it, there will still be a period of mourning, perhaps quite a long period. The best advice I can give you is to be as *unkind* as necessary. Repeat the facts again and again. Maybe fabricate evidence to 'prove' that he's dead. But, do it soon, and persevere until she is able to say she knows James is dead".

"And there are no drugs to help in the process?" Sir Charles was unsure of his ability to carry out such a distasteful task.

"I'm afraid not. Tranquillizers would be no use. In fact, they would prolong the agony. She may need a traumatic shock, not gentle words, and such a shock can only come from someone she trusts".

Sir Charles left the doctor's surgery in somber mood. It had been a month since James' disappearance, and in that time more and more evidence had accumulated that James had been the victim of an elaborate trap. The tampering of the telephone lines from his base to Woodvale had been confirmed. He had been deliberately lured away so that James could not contact him about the mission he was required to carry out. He did not know what the mission was, and all who could have given information in this matter had disappeared or had been killed in the attack on the local Resistance.

Nor had the discovery, at Wright's apartment, of forged documents and equipment thrown any light on the possible objective of James' mission. Sir Charles had become more and more puzzled. Why would the Germans endanger the position of Wright, admittedly not highly placed, but placed in the War Office nevertheless, to capture an individual British Commando who might not be in a position to give information? A possible explanation of this had arisen in the last few days, when Sir Charles received an intelligence briefing that Stockhausen was, in fact, still alive. It seems the story of his death, probably planted by Wright, had been used to induce in James and Sir Charles a sense of security. Combined with the liquidation of the Calais Resistance, the re-emergence of Stockhausen finally dispelled any lingering hopes Sir Charles had that James might be a prisoner of war. Not so for Charlotte, who refused to accept what was clear to everyone else. Even the inevitable War Office telegram 'missing, presumed dead', had not shaken her belief.

Immediately upon his arrival at Bishop's Lodge, Sir Charles telephoned the vicar.
After a lengthy conversation, he put down the telephone. He took his address book from the desk and began a long series of telephone calls, thus preparing the ground for his first attack on his daughter's implacable belief.

Charlotte arrived home at 6.30pm, as usual. At the request of Sir Charles, the matron had ensured that she had been given only light duties that day, and her dismissal a few minutes earlier than normal allowed her to miss the inevitable rush. She arrived home in as relaxed a condition as was possible, with no further stresses imposed that day by her nursing experiences.

"Hello, darling. I've arrange for a memorial service to be held a week on Saturday, and I've invited all the people who had enquired about such a service, and several others who would want to attend. You're not working on that Saturday, I know". Sir Charles hoped that he sounded matter of fact.

"A memorial service? For whom?" She looked at her father with vacant eyes, genuinely surprised.

Sir Charles pursed his lips and lowered his eyes. He was determined to remain calm, however long it took. Even so, when he eventually spoke, there was the slightest hint of frustration. "It's a way of enabling us all to pay our last respects to James. Afterwards a few of them will be coming back here for a few drinks and a buffet".

"But why should we have a *memorial* service?" Her demeanor was childlike, but there was no antagonism in her voice.

"Because James has been killed, Charlotte". Although the words almost choked him, he tried to sound matter of fact. He watched her as she lowered her eyes and began gently to shake her head. "Charlotte. All the evidence points to this. It is overwhelming. You must accept it, must come to terms with it. Life has to go on". He paused, and then said, stressing each word to emphasize their finality. "James is dead."

She looked up at the wall, her mouth and eyes opening slightly wider momentarily. A tear trickled from her eye.

23rd October. North Germany

The wind was bitingly cold and James was chilled to the bone. He had been robbed of his coat and shoes two days earlier and had torn up his tablecloth to wrap around his feet. At times he had been jostled and trampled underfoot as people around him stampeded. Now he was seated, undecided about his next move. He had noticed a dramatic increase in temperature for a while, but that was hours ago. The warmth had now gone, to be replaced by this mind-numbing cold. As he huddled behind what he believed was a large chunk of masonry, he felt from within the warm glow of elation. He was sure there had been an air-raid. This, weeks after Stockhausen had said the Allies would sue for peace within days, meant that England was still fighting. Even in his miserable condition he was able to smile at his thoughts; workers in the munitions factories, the doctors and nurses, the troops with their banter and complaining, all working, straining every muscle and sinew to rid the world of the scourge of Nazism. And Charlotte, healthy, unscarred, unburned and secure. Stockhausen must have lied about an attack on London. He had probably lied about everything. It was only a matter of time before the inevitable Allied victory, and then peacetime conditions would start to return; help for the vulnerable, food, shelter. All he had to do was survive the terrible months ahead.

The Army would have given up hope of finding him. Even Sir Charles. But Charlotte would not. She could not know where he was; she could not know his condition; but she would know he was alive. She would pray, hope and believe, and this gave him strength and courage. Starving and freezing, he nevertheless smiled, certain of the awesome power of her love.

Saturday 4th November England

They filed slowly out of the small, picturesque village church. The vicar had spoken in compassionate terms about the men who had lost their lives in the War, with particular reference to Lieutenant James Courtney. At the reception at Bishop's Lodge, Sir Charles kept a watchful eye on his daughter. She was busying herself in the role of hostess, making sure everyone had a drink and sandwiches. She was mingling easily with those who had come to pay their last respects to

James; Simon and his fiancee; Henri, with some officers from Holmbury; a number of officers from Sir Charles' base who had known and worked with James; several neighbors and local people from the village; and a number of tenant farmers from Sir Charles' estate. The mood was subdued, as befitted the occasion, but Sir Charles was becoming more optimistic. At least his daughter was reacting to people, talking, and comforting them as necessary, and receiving their sympathy and best wishes in return. Her previous, mildly catatonic state had been replaced by something that he recognized as his daughter, lively, animated, confident.

Finally, the last of the guests had gone. As they were clearing away the crockery, Sir Charles said. "Rather more turned up than I expected"

"Yes". She smiled faintly.

"It was quite a touching service, don't you think?"

"Mmmm".

He was pleased. Perhaps this stratagem would do the trick, this symbolic laying-to-rest of James, this commending of his soul to God's protection. Perhaps she would now start to pay serious attention to her life and future. Gently, he took her hands in his. "Charlotte, I was very pleased at the dignified way you acted today. I was very proud".

She stopped what she was doing and looked at him. "In a new situation, however difficult or painful, people learn to cope. They accept what has happened, and learn to cope with it, and they carry on and do their best. And in the end, it all comes right".

Sir Charles heard the words, but the faraway look in her eyes told him she was not talking to him, merely thinking aloud. What he could not know was that she was not even talking about herself. She was talking about someone very, very special.

Friday 10th November

It was still an hours' drive to Bishop's Lodge; he could still call off the whole plan. Even when it had first been suggested he was not certain that he wanted to go through with the deceit, but doctor Young's arguments had been so convincing, and all other approaches had so far been notably unsuccessful. Reluctantly, he had agreed. Certainly, given the continuing situation with Charlotte, something drastic was needed. There had seemed to be a marked improvement from the days just after James' death, the days of somber introspection and debilitating indolence. She had been out with friends to dances and parties. She had almost been back to her normal self, and then the truth slipped out.

It was on the day when the people on the neighboring estate, who had actually been James' legal guardians, brought over his personal belongings. They felt it would be appropriate for Charlotte to have them. Amongst other things were several items of good quality clothing. Sir Charles assumed that she would donate these to some charitable cause; heaven knew, there was certainly a shortage of clothing in England in 1944.

Charlotte had washed and pressed everything. Her father asked if she knew who would be able to make the best use of them. The question had been asked with no intention beyond simple inquiry, but her reply stunned him. She said that James would need them *when he got home.*

When Dr. Young heard of this he became very concerned. Every report he had received from Sir Charles seemed to indicate improvement, acceptance of James' death, a moving on in life for Charlotte, but this showed that she was still clinging to the belief that James was alive. After consulting with colleagues Young advised Sir Charles that the next step should be to provide an eye-witness to tell her personally that he had seen James' dead body. If no such person could be found, then one would have to be fabricated. The deceit would be worth it if it enabled Charlotte to move on in her life. Sir Charles had spoken of this to Henri, who agreed with the plot and promised to enlist the help of one of his most trusted Resistance friends. It was this man who now sat beside Sir Charles in the car. Henri had agreed to concoct a story, based on known details, with credible embellishments, which his friend, whose name was Jean Dubois, would tell to Charlotte.

The car swept majestically through the gates of Bishop's Lodge and came to a halt behind Charlotte's little car at the front of the house. Sir Charles instructed the driver to wait in order to return Dubois to London. Charlotte was sitting in the drawing room, reading.

"Hello Daddy. Who is it you want me to meet?"

"Hello Darling. Charlotte, this is Jean Dubois, one of the few surviving members of the Calais Resistance. He came over to London recently to provide our intelligence boys with information regarding German formations and morale. One of the people questioning him told me that he might be able to tell us something about James' last mission. When I interviewed him he was able to fill in some of the blank spaces in the story. When he discovered you were James' fiancee he very kindly agreed to come here and tell you what he knows. But I warn you, it's not very pleasant"

Charlotte looked at Dubois. He was much the same build as James, and his soft brown eyes and boyishness gave him an air of innocence and simplicity. She felt immediately that she could trust him.

"Please, Mr. Dubois, sit down and tell me what you know".

"Miss Charlotte, I live with my parents on a small farm near Calais. Most of our living comes from the herd of dairy cows which we breed. They are amongst the best in the whole of France. This gives me the opportunity to wander around almost at will. If ever I'm questioned, I tell them I am looking for missing cattle. Very early in September I was bringing in the cows for milking when I saw a very unusual sight. It was a military roadblock on the main road to Calais. Even more surprising is that it wasn't the ordinary army. It was the SS. I quickly returned home and told my father. He told me to go straight back, conceal myself, and watch what happened. In the mean-time he would go to Calais and inform the Resistance leaders. When I returned, the local priests' cart had been stopped. The priest was curled up on the grass. After the SS left I went down to the scene. The priest was dead, a bullet to the head, but there was another man also. It turned out that this was an Englishman, an agent well known to the Resistance, who had been many times to help us in our struggle. He stayed a few times at our farm. I knew his face well, but I did not know his name. It was that man there". Dubois pointed to a photograph on the mantle-piece, a portrait of James. Charlotte looked at the photograph and then back at Dubois. He continued. "He was dressed in the clothes of a local farmer, so he would not have been taken as a prisoner of war. I'm sorry I have to tell you this; there were several bullets in his body. He must have died instantly, with little pain. I heard the sound of a truck approaching, so I had to hide. I watched the regular army come and take away both bodies. There is no doubt in my mind that both the priest and the Englishman were dead".

There was silence in the room. Sir Charles looked at his daughter, who looked at Dubois and, indicating James' photograph said, "And you are certain it was this man".

"Absolutely. I knew his face well from his days spent at our farm. There was just not time to bring help".

Again, there was silence, a heavy, oppressive stillness, an interlude whilst she absorbed the bitter information. Sir Charles watched her discreetly. She sat quite still, betraying no emotion on her face, in her eyes. At last she looked directly at Dubois. "Thank you, Mr. Dubois It cannot have been easy for you to relive this awful thing, but you have set my mind at rest. Thank you very much. You will stay for tea?"

"Thank you, but I cannot" He stood up and smiled at her. "I am expected back in London as soon as possible. Hopefully we will meet again under happier circumstances". With this he shook her hand and took his leave.

Sir Charles showed him to the door and gave the driver the address at which Dubois was staying. He leaned through the window and spoke in a low voice. "Thank you, Dubois. You have done a good day's work today. If ever I can be of help, don't hesitate to let me know".

"Thank you, Sir Charles. Good luck".

When he returned to the drawing room Charlotte had resumed reading her book.

This greatly encouraged Sir Charles. The doctor had said there would be no great show of emotion if she accepted the story. That would come later, in private. The name of Dubois was never mentioned again by either of them.

That night, as usual since James' disappearance, Charlotte cried herself to sleep. And, as usual since that fateful day, James came to her in the secret, private world of her dreams. In this world they were still lovers; the passion, as great as ever; the dreams, as real as ever; the hopes, as possible as ever. And when he left her, always the same words; believe; be constant. He always faded, wraith-like, into a foggy void. After the meeting with Dubois, the image faded more quickly, his words increasingly urgent, as her hope and belief grew weaker, until, finally, on Christmas eve, 1944, an event occurred which transformed the situation.

Midnight 24/25th December 1944 Hamburg

Karin Wecker stood in the shadows beneath the railway arch which had become her domain. Tonight, for the first time in weeks, the street light was actually illuminated, throwing distorted, spectral shadows onto the slimy walls. She shuddered as she surveyed her surroundings. Memories flooded back, as they did every night, of happier times, her life before the folly of this war.

She and her husband had been blessed with high academic qualifications, he as a doctor and she as the chief translator for a major exporting company. Their two children had shown much promise in their early days at school. Being, themselves, the only offspring of their own highly successful parents meant that they had enjoyed a privileged upbringing, with a substantial inheritance in due course. The World had seemed their oyster, especially as German national confidence and self-respect grew in the 1930s. They had had a beautiful home, and had travelled abroad extensively, a practice that was still the privilege of the few.

How things had changed! Her husband had been killed in the first year of the war, shortly after the death in quick succession of their parents on both sides of the family. With no close relatives to turn to, she had to rely on her own powers and experience. She had, however, enjoyed a privileged and protected environment all her life; she was completely unprepared to face a world of harsh reality, especially when that reality was total warfare. As the course of events went increasingly against Germany, her prospects similarly degenerated. Her own children died in 1942, the boy from influenza, and the girl from injuries sustained during an air-raid. Her house was completely destroyed in the same incident, and all the contents, furniture, valuables, even her clothes, were lost. In subsequent months and years, as the situation deteriorated further, civilization largely broke down. Society approached a condition she described as feral. Any kindness and compassion she had tried to show to her fellow civilians was rewarded by trickery, cheating and bad faith. It had become a battle merely to stay alive, where the survival of one person was dependent on their ability to deprive another of the means of life. She had been constantly tricked and cheated by so-called friends and neighbors.

Now, there was only one person who mattered. She had no notion of morality; no sense of other people's rights; no sense of self-respect. Her only goal was her own survival. She had now tricked, cheated and stolen, from, especially, the weak and vulnerable. Everyone was now her enemy. She would do anything to obtain the smallest advantage. She had given her body to scores of men in return for anything which might improve her material condition. If they came to her drunk, so much the better, so much easier was it to rob them. She relished the possibilities when people, men or women, young or old, showed kindness. It was a weakness she had expunged from her own personality, and one she had learned to exploit. She was utterly vicious, ruthless and unscrupulous.

Tonight looked unpromising. A figure had entered into view, an old man, with long, matted beard and hair. He stumbled along as if barley able to place one foot in front of the other. Good; if necessary, she would use violence against him, if she could just engineer the right approach. Even pathetic specimens like this would have some crumbs of value, and in today's circumstances, crumbs were all that was likely to be on offer. As he came closer, she noticed he was carrying a stick. He was tapping the wall as he went along; he was blind. That was even better, he was even more vulnerable. When he was near enough, she called out. "Want some company tonight, Sir?" There was no reply. Nor was there a reply when she repeated the question. He was deaf as well. She picked up a half brick from the side of the road. She would smash his head and take whatever was of use whilst he was unconscious, and if she hit him too hard, well, who would miss this old tramp. She rushed towards him, a malevolent snarl distorting her face. Only a few feet away now, almost in reach of her prize, she suddenly stopped in her tracks. Her intended victim continued his painful journey. Had she heard what *she feared above all? Surely, that had not been the sound she dreaded. She dropped the brick and rushed back to the wall, to the shadow which was her only protection. She cursed her luck. She would now lose whatever this unfortunate creature had, to the animals approaching him now.*

19.00 hours 24th December Bishops Lodge

Sir Charles looked at himself in the full-length mirror. He had to admit to himself that the years had been good to him. He could still cut a dash with the ladies, especially in his dress uniform. The annual Christmas Ball for regimental officers was his favorite event of the year. True, attendance had been erratic for the last few years, for obvious reasons. But now, the favorable situation at the Front meant that there should be a good turn out tonight, especially as they had taken the opportunity during recent years to invite officers from other regiments, resulting, naturally, in reciprocal invitations.

There was a knock at the bedroom door. "Come in". It was Charlotte, of course, there being nobody else in the house. She swept into the room in a white ball gown. It was a dress she had made herself. Heaven knows where she had obtained the material. He never ceased to be amazed at the ability of women to produce things from the least promising raw materials.

"Charlotte. You look lovely. I'll have the belle of the ball with me tonight"

"And I'll have the handsomest escort"

He smiled at her and looked at his watch. It would take about an hour to get to the venue where the event was taking place, a large hotel in Regent St., in Central London, chosen for its large ballroom and the lack of bomb damage to the building. Sir Charles had booked rooms for himself and Charlotte, and one of the drivers had taken their luggage earlier. The doorbell chimed. "That'll be the car. Are you ready?" he asked his daughter. A few minutes later they were on their way to London.

They made good time, so it was just before eight when they entered the ballroom.

Several of the younger officers approached, and, after paying due respect to Sir Charles, asked Charlotte to dance. The result was that she danced for an hour before rejoining her father at their table. A number of other officers came over to pay their respects, and mindful of James' death and Charlotte's sorrow, were careful to avoid mention of their late comrade.

After a while, Charlotte and her father made their way to the buffet table. Even in these times of rationing plenty of salad was available. As her father loaded his plate, Charlotte noticed a solitary figure at the bar. She froze, as if gripped by an invisible vice. Standing at the bar was James. She had seen his face only for a brief moment, and then only in profile, but there was no doubt about it. It was his nose, his eyes, his mouth. Now that his back was turned to her, she could see it was his build, his body.

By now her father had turned around and joined her. He, too, was looking towards the bar, and he was saying something to her, small talk, something inconsequential. She could not understand why he was making insignificant comments. Couldn't he see? It was James, missing for months. It was the man she loved. Standing there, ten yards away.

Hamburg

Werewolves. The most feral of the feral; the vicious of the vicious. The low, ominous, threatening whistle was their trademark. It was this sound that had so alarmed Karin as she rushed to attack James. From her hiding place she could hear their oaths and drunken laughter. Soon, they would be in sight. There were thought to be thousands of them, disaffected, bitter, sullen German youths, most with rudimentary military training, deserters who banded together in small, informal groups, with no command structure, no discipline, no ethical leanings; the scum of a scum-ridden society. It was their perverse intention to inflict more misery onto a society which they saw as the authors of their plight. They were not the patriots, the freedom fighters, or the heroes that they were intended to be when the idea of a partisan force was first mooted. They were merely a rabble, thugs who preyed on the weak and defenseless. On this bitterly cold winter night their paths were destined to cross that of James Courtney.

Karin saw them enter the archway from the far end. She crouched further back, desperate to remain unseen. There were four of them, none older than fifteen, drunk, with vicious, sunken eyes, and skeletal heads. So immersed were they in their own vulgarity that it seemed they would not notice the old man. He might have escaped, undetected, had he not at that moment tripped over a large piece of masonry. As it was, one of the werewolves noticed him and called out something Karin could not hear clearly. There was silence as they awaited his reply. He struggled to his feet and continued on his way, apparently ignoring the youths. The four surrounded him and repeated their inane comments. Again, there was no reply. Suddenly, the one who had spoken first slapped James' face. The victim stopped but made no reply. By now they must have realized that he was deaf and blind. Karin shuddered as she considered his prospects over the next few minutes. She knew that his best course of action was to submit immediately. That would ensure that his punishment was kept to a minimum.

One of the four, too dense to care that the non-response was due to deafness and blindness, grabbed James and pushed him into the arms of another. He, in turn, threw James to one of the others, so that James was pushed around in a circle, as the werewolves enjoyed a grim joke. Karin felt nauseated as she witnessed the degrading spectacle. Something then happened that was to change her life. The victim grasped one of his assailants and lashed out with his fist. The blow caught the youth just below the temple and sent him sprawling to the ground. A second moved in to attack but played into James' hands by trying to grapple with him. James seized him and winded him with a blow to the stomach. A second punch to the chin lifted him off the ground and deposited him, like a rag doll, in the slush. Sadly, the outcome would be the worse for James, who could not make an escape. Soon, the four would reform and take bloody revenge for this humiliation. But in Karin's heart was the spark of a long-forgotten emotion. It had been a long time since she had been in the presence of someone whom she could respect and admire. This brave man, who must have known that he was up against overwhelming odds, had nevertheless fought to save his pride. A tear came to her eye as the sensation tingled up and down her spine. She looked at the man, no longer a shuffling wreck, but an example of courage worthy of respect. He did not try to run or hide; did not cower. He stood, almost majestically, facing this unseen enemy.

They circled around him, wary, screaming abuse. Now, they were fully aware of his defenselessness. One of them approached him from the side and punched him in the face. This was the signal for the others to attack. James was easily beaten to the ground. Karin winced as blow after blow fell upon him. She could not know that their drunkenness reduced the effectiveness of their attack. It was less severe than others James had suffered recently. Even so, he was battered into semi-consciousness. They tore off his coat and jacket, and his woolen pullover and his shoes. Their bloodlust satisfied, they left him there. As they walked away, rejoicing in this latest 'victory', they threw his clothes over the road. It would be difficult, to say the least, for a blind man to find them. Semi-naked, James would freeze to death in a very short time.

London

Sir Charles was puzzled. Three times he had asked her the same question and had received no reply. She had simply stared straight ahead, wide-eyed, open-mouthed, with an uncomprehending fascination on her face. He had looked in the same direction and could see nothing which might cause this strange reaction.

"James!" She had spoken the word as quietly as breathing.

"James". Louder, now. Intense.

"James". This time, the word was roared. Sir Charles, unaffected by the vision of James Courtney his daughter had seen, looked dumbly at her. She dropped her plate and glass and rushed across the dance floor. She barged into two couples, who in turn disturbed others. She collided with a waiter, who dropped a full tray of drinks with a crash. The band stopped playing. By now, everyone was looking towards the source of the commotion. Sir Charles, horrified, put down his glass and set off after his daughter. She knocked over a table. Food and drink were splashed over the people sitting there. A woman screamed. Charlotte was oblivious to all this. She only knew that in a few moments she would be in the arms of her beloved James, now just an arm's length away. She did not care that he had not been in touch; explanations could wait. She felt no anger, just a wild, exulting passion. She reached out and grasped his muscular arm. As he turned around in response, she looked into the face of a complete stranger.

Hamburg

It must have been at least ten or fifteen minutes. If she did not move soon, the man would be dead. If she moved too soon, and attracted the attention of the werewolves, they would both die. She crept from her hiding place as soon as the werewolves were nowhere to be seen. This did not mean that they were not there, hiding, skulking. No matter. This was one of those times when a risk had to be taken in a noble cause. She had not felt like this for years. She quickly gathered James' clothes as she approached the prostrate figure.

The cold was numbing and he knew that he would soon have to make some sort of effort. Then he noticed it; the slightest whiff of perfume. There was a woman nearby; potentially a far more lethal threat than the assailants of a few minute ago, but possibly, also, an angel. Could it possibly be...? He dismissed the thought immediately. It was wishful thinking. He felt a soft hand on his brow. He resisted the impulse to make a response. Better to let her commit herself to a course of action before responding himself. She was pulling him, lifting him, helping him get to his feet. He was too cold to notice the benefit immediately, but he knew that she was putting clothes onto his body. She was a friend. At last. She put his stick into his hand and wrapped his arm around her shoulder and tried to support him. His massive frame dwarfed her small woman's body.

It would take half an hour to get him back to her home. There would be shelter, and a little food, enough to keep him alive for one more night. Tonight, he could sleep in her bed, and tomorrow she would prepare as best she could the corner of her semi derelict cellar that remained unused.

London

He had taken her to her room in the hotel. He had made what apologies he could, inadequate, inevitably, in the circumstances. Now, he would have to grasp the nettle. After weeks of apparent progress, the truth had been revealed. She clung, still, to James' memory. In her own interests, for her own good, for the sake of her mental health, he would resort to the last option.

"You stupid young woman". On the word 'stupid', he slapped her face. "You've shown yourself up. Do you think you are the only one who loved James? We all did. We all feel remorse. But everyone else accepts the facts. But you? You grasp to straws. You cling to fantasies" He held her shoulders in his hands, shaking her. He was scornful, snarling. "You must accept the fact that James is dead. He's dead. Dead!" At this last word he threw her onto the bed. Heartbroken and sickened by what he had done, he left her and retired, weeping, to his room.

She lay, crying, on the bed for several minutes. She had been so sure, so sure, but, in fact, he was nothing like James. She was shocked that she had embarrassed him, a complete stranger, and her father. She sobbed pitifully, until she was hardly able to breathe. She looked at herself in the mirror on the dressing table. Her face was blotchy and streaked with tears. She blew her nose, took a deep breath, and forced herself to look at her reflection until she stopped crying. She repeated out loud, again and again "James is dead". Again, her tears flowed.

Charlotte's mind was devastated by the realization, now, of what had happened. Her heart was filled with fear and trepidation, as the golden future she had believed she and James were destined to share now dissolved into a dry, arid, lifeless desert. Wave upon wave of despair swept over her. It seemed to her that her life was useless and futile. She knew she would never love again as she had loved James.

For Charlotte Crayne, this moment was the most desolate and wretched of her life.

Hamburg

Karin struggled with the arduous task of supporting weight of this stranger. Finally, they reached the comparative safety of her home. She would now devote herself to the protection of this other person, and not only to her own needs, however pressing the circumstances were.

For Karin Wecker, in her wretched, desolate home, this was the moment of the rebirth of her humanity.

Part 2

Chapter 18

Mile after mile of desolation. Everywhere she looked Charlotte could see shattered buildings. Gas mains, electricity cables, water mains, sewage pipes, all damaged. Makeshift hospitals, temporary shelters fashioned from random bits of wood and sheets of corrugated iron, and endless queues. These were the visual manifestations of defeat. At first there had been resentful acceptance of occupation, following the surrender in May 1945. Initially, there had also been a willingness to oppose instructions from the military and even misguided attempts at sabotage. This changed very quickly when it was pointed out to the population that winter was only a few months away, and they would perish or survive according to their own efforts. Very few who were lucky enough to have survived the conflict now relished the possibility of freezing to death. Ordinary Germans were clearing rubble, working feverishly, often with bare hands, desperate to improve their condition before the onset of the cold. Weary, starving and crushed, haunted by almost daily revelations of the atrocities carried out by their compatriots, the people of Germany stooped to salvage something of their national pride.

It was now September 1945. Germany's unconditional surrender had come in May. The general war in Europe was over. Other, minor regional conflicts would rumble on for a short while, as would the war in Japan, but the perception of the British people was that hostilities were over and that victory had been achieved. Now came the problems of post war reconstruction. The sights she had witnessed had convinced Charlotte that there could be no reasonably civilized life in Europe for years to come. At least thirty million people had perished; too many of these had been in the economically productive age group. Factories, hospitals, schools, water mains, roads, bridges, railway systems, all smashed. Doctors, nurses, medicine, food, clothing, everything was in short supply. America alone had the intact infrastructure to supply so many essentials, and America was already operating at record, unsustainable levels. The figures of the logistical problems were overwhelming. The statistics of armies had been mind-boggling; supplies and provisions for three million men! How could it be done? Now, people were talking about supplies and provisions for a whole continent.

Charlotte sat back in her seat as the car picked its way slowly through the ruined streets. She resolved, again, to think it through logically, but again her mind was swamped by her first thought. The people of Germany needed twenty million loaves of bread. Not in the few months it would take to build a bakery; not in the ten months it would take to grow and collect a harvest of wheat. They needed them now, today. And again tomorrow. She tried to picture twenty million loaves of bread, and twenty million eggs, and twenty million pints of milk. To Germany's woes she added Italy and Greece, France, Belgium, Holland, even Britain, the victor. The goods simply were not available. The problems seemed insurmountable. And this first problem, these first difficulties, the solution of which she could not even conceive, were the problems of mere survival. She dared not even think about improving the quality of life.

"I know what you're thinking." Her father's voice woke her from her reverie. She looked at him, his face a knowing, kindly smile. "You can't believe that life can ever return to something approaching normality." She looked out of the window into the streets. He continued, "But you're wrong. People will pick themselves up again. It'll be a hard, grinding task, but it may surprise you to know that the Germans are amongst the best in the World to cope with that task. They are hard-working, industrious Teutons, easily regimented and organized, ideal for rebuilding from scratch. Mark my words, with the right men and women in charge Germany will be transformed within ten years."

It was hard to believe but believe it she must. Her father had been proved right in recent months in so many of his predictions, from the defeat of Churchill in the general election to the defeat, in the awesome, searing heat of the atom bomb, of Japan.

"It just seems there is so much to do." She shook her head slowly as she spoke these words. At that point the car slowed and came to a halt.

"We'd better let the troop-carrier catch up Sir. It wouldn't do to be left isolated around here." The driver's advice was sound common sense. Sir Charles looked through the back window. Shortly, the escort came into view. The driver restarted the engine and continued the journey.

"Yes, there is." He was addressing his daughter again. "But it's not as bad everywhere in Germany as it is here. Some parts have been all but untouched by the War. In the South there are vineyards and orchards yielding wines and fruits exactly as they have done for years. Butter and cheese are being made, cattle milked, crops and vegetables gathered in just as usual. The problems are not quite as bad as they seem"

"But look out of the window. There are people dressed in rags. No tents, no blankets. No prospects. No hope."

"That's right. There is certainly deprivation. Some will die of starvation. Some will freeze to death. But the overall picture, in terms of how much stuff is needed and how much is available, is not as bad as it seems here. Don't forget, this city was a major port and industrial center. It had a thousand bombers sent against it several times. It was a vital strategic target. That's why there is so much devastation."

Indeed, it had been a vital part of the German war effort. Through this port had come millions of tons of iron ore for armaments. This had certainly been a major target. They were driving into the city of Hamburg.

Chapter 19

"You've made much better time than we anticipated, Charles." The speaker was the Commanding Officer of British forces in the Hamburg sector. "So much the better for me. I haven't been home since D-Day and I can tell you I'm really looking forward to the next few weeks."

Sir Charles was lounging in a large wicker chair. For his part, he certainly was *not* looking forward to the next few weeks. Soon after the surrender he had been put in charge of the security of all British military installations in the British sector of occupied Germany. It had proved an arduous and boring task. Some Germans had tried to form a Resistance movement against the occupying Allies. This soon petered out, but a few had continued guerrilla warfare. There had been several nasty incidents before they were finally subdued.

"You must really be looking forward to seeing Marjorie and the children?" Sir Charles suggested.

"Yes indeed. You've got yours with you, haven't you?"

"Yes. She wanted to be involved in building a better world, as the young always do, and I wanted her near me so I could keep an eye on her". Sir Charles watched the other officer, who was now checking through some files. They had met at military academy in the early twenties and had kept in touch periodically, through mutual friends.

"The situation here is pretty routine now. The population has accepted defeat and got down fairly well to the job of getting back on their feet. There is very little vandalism, although, needless to say, still some anti-British feeling. In spite of this, it should be a piece of cake for the next few weeks." He paused to consider if any further information or advice needed to be passed on. "I believe you're being posted back to England when I return from leave."

"Yes. We've got to start drawing up plans for the next war against the Russkies." They both smiled wryly.

"Righto. I'll leave it with you and I'll see you in a couple of weeks." The two men shook hands and the C.O. left the office.

Sir Charles picked up the phone and gave instructions that his car should be available in one hour. He intended to drive across the city to inspect the damage at the docks. Leaving the office, he decided to stroll around the base which would be his home for the next two weeks. It was located just outside the city borders, as there were no suitable buildings left intact inside the city. The Royal Engineers had rapidly thrown up a barracks and a small field hospital. The latter included nurses' quarters where Charlotte would be staying. There were dozens of rows of tents, which acted as temporary accommodation for many of the six thousand troops in the immediate area. There were permanently at least one thousand troops in the city, on patrol or attached to what passed as police stations or municipal departments. He was glad that he would not have to get involved in planning decisions; this was just a holding operation until the C.O. returned.

He found Charlotte in the NAAFI (Navy, Army, Air Force Institutes; organizations which provided canteens, shops, etc for British military personnel), drinking tea with one of the other auxiliaries. He made a mental note that she had quickly made friends with someone. A very good sign, and one which the doctor at home would be pleased with. "I'm doing a tour of the city this afternoon to see what's what. Do you want to come?"

"They haven't assigned me any duties so far, so I might as well. When do we leave?"

"In about half an hour. Can you be at my office by then?"

"Yes. I'll get changed straight away." One hour later they were making slow but steady progress towards the center of Hamburg. The streets were clear of rubble and there were very few non-military vehicles. Lots of rickety bicycles were in evidence and the odd horse-drawn cart could be seen. The driver knew the area well, as did the lieutenant in the front seat who was giving Sir Charles as much information as possible.

As they approached the center of the city the number of people on the streets increased. British troops were constantly in view, questioning people, directing people. The car turned a corner onto a road which, the lieutenant had told them, would lead to the main market square. The driver braked suddenly, and the car came to a halt a few yards from the place where a cart had overturned. Troops and civilians were struggling to get it upright. The owner, a local trader, was feverishly collecting his pitifully few spilled goods. There would be several minutes' delay.

Idly looking out of the car window Charlotte noticed a slowly moving queue, at a soup kitchen, one of several she had seen in the last hour or so. Nearby was a group of children, playing with a ball, throwing it to each other, and racing to retrieve it when it was dropped. She marveled and was warmed by the resilience of children. One of them threw the ball with too much force. It bounced a few times and came to rest near the front of the queue. Several children rushed to regain ownership and in the headlong melee they bundled into the person at the front, causing the old man who had just been served to drop his bowl, the hot soup spilling and being lost on the pavement. The children melted into the crowd. Charlotte felt a twinge of pity for the man. She knew he would not be served again. Each person got one portion and no more. It would be hardship, but to go without food for one day would not kill him. Not a disaster, just a nuisance. She watched him grope, just fifty yards away, for his stick. He must be blind. Having retrieved the implement he stood up facing her, almost looking straight at her. She heard the driver start the engine. The cart was upright, the goods collected, and they would be able to resume their tour in a few moments. The old man who had lost his soup held his head as if looking at the sky; his left hand at his throat; his right hand on his hip; the weight of his body had shifted mainly onto his right leg; his left leg was bent at the knee. He stood completely still.

Charlotte sat, fascinated at this sight. There was no ranting or raving. No obvious sign of frustration. But frustration there must have been and this is how this old man deals with it. She had seen something similar before. This was similar to the way James had reacted at the tennis match which now overwhelmingly flooded into her memory. It was so similar, *so* similar. The car began to move. Such was the hold that this image had upon her that she had to turn her body around to keep the old man in view. Slowly, he began to recede as the car moved on. They turned a corner. The image was gone.

Shocked by the intensity of her feelings at this event, she sat back in her seat. Her breathing was heavy; she could feel the pounding of her heart. It seemed incredible; a reaction so similar to what James would have done in the same circumstances. So similar. So similar. She could not remove the word from her brain. So similar, if James had survived the war. But he had not survived, he had been lost. But this was so similar. In those circumstances. And even if James had survived, the chance that he was at that place, on that day, at that hour, with her so nearby, was a million to one. A million to one. And so similar. And like a revelation, it dawned on her. In fact, it was not similar. IT WAS IDENTICAL. But it was a million to one. A MILLION to one. The words raced through her mind IDENTICAL. MILLION. MILLION. MILLION. IDENTICAL. And if it was James in the queue, it was a million to one chance that she would see it. And she *was* that one in a million chance. Only her, only she in the entire world, her, she, one in a million. A one in a million chance, AND THE CHANCE WAS NOW.

The car screeched to a halt as the door was flung open. Before anyone could react Charlotte was racing down the road towards the market square. The three men in the car looked at each other, searching for a clue to this event. What on earth was going on? Why was she sprinting down the road like that? Sir Charles and the lieutenant leapt from the car and raced after her. She reached the market square and looked around, frantically searching the faces. She cursed her lack of German language. There were five streets leading off the square. He was nowhere in sight. *The man had gone.* She didn't notice that a group of Germans had started to gather around her; hostile, threatening. Her father and his officer arrived within moments and bundled her back to the car.

Chapter 20

It was lucky for Charlotte that the day was mild, not a harbinger of the months to come. What spoiled it was the rain. It was like Glasgow, or Manchester. These great British cities also were ports, or at least had a canal which gave access to the sea. They were also major industrial centers, just like here in Hamburg. The rain was not the soft, life-giving element, nor the thunderous, explosive torrents of nature's rage. This rain was just drenching, drizzling, endlessly depressing. It was raining when she woke that morning, and it was still raining now. She was completely wet from head to toe. She was grateful that the temperature did not add to her misery. She was also grateful that the German cleaner at the hospital had had clothes that fitted her, insubstantial though they were. This way she would remain inconspicuous.

The market square was exactly as it had been the previous day, but the man she was waiting for had not turned up. She had arrived in time to see the soup kitchen being set up by large German women, all bustle and efficiency, their hair in a bun, their clothing functional, surprisingly jovial, given the circumstances. They had been serving for hours, while she stood, and watched, and waited. Her thoughts strayed back to the previous night. She had persuaded one of the nurses to use her influence with one of the army drivers to get her a lift to the market square this morning and back to the base in the evening. The arrangement was that she would remain on this spot and the driver would return each hour, on the hour, but ignore her unless she gave a pre-arranged signal. At that signal he would pick her up and return to base. She pointed out that there may be a man with her for the return journey. Five times the driver had returned; five hours with no shelter from the rain.

The previous day's 'fiasco', to use her father's word, had resulted, needless to say, in an interrogation. She had used the simple tactic of complete silence, to buy time, to think. Finally, she had put the incident down to 'feminine circumstances', an excuse which immediately brought an end to the questioning, without even a 'don't do it again'. She had admitted that a lone British military person, especially a woman, would be very vulnerable in the circumstances into which she had put herself, and this, combined with an air of contrition, had satisfied Sir Charles. She knew that she had to choose the right time to tell him of her suspicion that James was alive and nearby.

It was now getting late in the afternoon. By this time yesterday they had returned to the base. She was beginning to lose hope when the man suddenly appeared, shuffling towards the queue, bowl in hand. The market square was bustling, but for Charlotte there was no noise or movement, except for this one man. His slow progress was arrested, as he reached the queue, by a hand from one of those already in the line. He was guided to his place at the end. Finally, he was served, and he turned to face Charlotte. He walked in her direction, carefully balancing the bowl of broth. He was walking directly towards her, until his stick found a lamp-post which her eyes had missed. He leaned against it and slowly drank the soup. Charlotte approached him. She stood a few feet from him. Despite the beard and long hair, and the bedraggled appearance, she could tell. There was no doubt about it; it was beyond question. It was certainly, definitely James.

Human emotions are notoriously unpredictable. Weak men can become heroes; friends can be seduced by expediency; love can be fickle. Charlotte stood before James, confronted by a situation which, only thirty hours ago, would have seemed impossible. Yet she was conscious of no tidal wave of love, nor of relief, nor even of pity, just the feeling that there was a duty to be performed, an undeclared vow to be honored. She quickly put the thought from her mind, for James had moved. She decided to follow him to establish his domestic situation.

The place which served as home was a hundred yards away. That explained his rapid disappearance the previous day. It was a narrow street with makeshift shelters on either side. She watched him pause at a railing and make his way down some steps into what remained of a basement. She drew level with the railing in time to see him open a door and enter. He closed the ill-fitting door with some difficulty. She noted the street name and house number. As quietly as possible she descended the steps. The door was of the part-glazed type, but all the glass had been smashed and any remaining fragments removed. She gently knocked at the door. After a few moments, she knocked again, this time much more loudly, so that he must hear....unless...... A wave of revulsion flowed through her as the realization dawned of what might have happened to him. She pushed the door, which opened with a creaking, scraping sound. This alone would be proof of the condition of his hearing. She saw him, slouched, unperturbed on a mattress. So, blind and deaf! There was a large window facing the street. This too had no glass. The room was tiny; James would have been able to touch all the walls if he had stood in the middle. It was very light, so that all parts of the room were clearly visible. There were cracks in all the walls and rain was evident in two places, dripping through what passed for a roof. On the floor were a threadbare mattress and one dirty sheet. A few mice scurried across the concrete, disturbed by James' return. There was an evil smell everywhere. Charlotte shuddered. On the wall opposite the door she could see where he had scraped something. To her it was unmistakable; with its' tower, and the shape of the window, it was a rough reproduction of Bishops' Lodge.

She had been aware that her arrival so suddenly might produce an unexpected shock for him, so she had previously wanted to be careful how she introduced herself, but that had changed. She would get him out of this hell now, immediately.

"James. It's me, Charlotte." He was sitting upright on the mattress, leaning against the wall. There was no reply, no reaction. She repeated her words. Again, no response. It dawned on her like a thunderbolt. This is what it means to be blind and deaf. At last, a wave of emotion swept through her as she realized what horrors he must have endured, even though she knew that she had shared them with him before.

Gently, she touched his ankle. His body became rigid and his breathing stopped. His hand slid under the edge of the mattress and he pulled out a rusty bayonet. He lashed out, missing her by inches. She recoiled, shocked, and stood up. He clambered to his feet. By the time he reached the door she was on the steps. In one leap she was in the street. He was only a few feet behind her, flailing and lashing in all directions. She ran along the narrow passage to safety. He stood on the top step brandishing the bayonet, grunting, snarling, like a wild animal protecting its lair. Trembling, with head bowed, she made her way back to the square. She resumed her position in anticipation of the arrival of the driver. Still the rain fell, but she was oblivious to it, and to her own discomfort.

The trip back to the base would take about an hour. She quickly stifled conversation with the driver in order to give her full attention to the problem of the moment. By the time she had reached the nurses' quarters her decision was made. Whatever the cost, whatever the pain, she would fight to restore James. She would not grow weary; she would not lose heart. In her mind, the decision was set in stone. She would not abandon him.

Chapter 21

Sir Charles was expecting her at 7pm. The note he had received late in the afternoon had stated that she wanted to see him in private. Charlotte had hoped that she would be able to present James to him, but things had not quite worked out that way. Sir Charles sat in his office quite unaware of, and unprepared for, the events of the next two hours.

A hot bath, a change of clothes and a good meal had worked their magic, and Charlotte's battered morale had been replaced by cautious optimism. This interview, however, had to be handled carefully. Her father might react angrily to the sound of James' name, let alone her claims that she had actually spent time with him. The things they had told her about James' 'death' were untrue. The story told by Dubois was a fabrication. However, she had already forgiven her father, for his intention, as always, had her best interests at heart. But, he could be expected to argue the point, unable to accept what she now *knew* to be the truth, that James was alive. The conversation might be frustrating. If she became angry, she might become hysterical. If that happened, her father had the power to have her sedated and returned to England. She could wake up in 24 hours in a hospital in London. In that case, the chances against rescuing James would increase a thousand-fold. She had settled on a course of action; she may have to do something she had never done before, never even contemplated. Above all, in this highly charged atmosphere, she must remain calm.

"Hello Daddy."

"Hello. What have you done today?"

"Oh, just looking around the city."

"Window shopping, eh?" He smiled. Her heart ached at the thought of what she might have to do. She returned his smile.

"Daddy, I've something very important to tell you, and a favor to ask." She produced an envelope from her handbag. "There's a piece of paper in this envelope on which an address is written, and a brief description of a basement dwelling in Hamburg. In that dwelling is a man and I want you to arrest him and bring him back to this hospital."

"What's he done?"

"He hasn't done anything, but he's a British subject and he's in need of medical attention."

"Charlotte, I can't arrest a man who has not broken the law just because I've got the power to do so. We've just fought a war against that kind of thing. Anyway, who is he and how do you know him?" She could feel tears filling her eyes. Control. She must keep self-control.

"Daddy, you know I love you and I would never do anything to hurt you. But this is so important to me." She paused to control her breathing. "Daddy, the man is James Courtney." She sensed immediately the fall in temperature, the change in atmosphere. This, she had expected. Her father seemed to age visibly before her. Her heart bled from the pain he was going through. He must think all the therapy was in vain, a hopeless cause. He must feel he had lost his daughter forever to a ghost.

"Charlotte. James is dead." He spoke quietly, patiently. Each word, spoken firmly, was a further burden on her shoulders. She felt frustration rising; there was danger. She must act on her plan immediately, before it was too late.

"Forgive me, father." Taking a deep breath, summoning up all her strength, she slapped her father across his face.

He sat quite still, shocked and stunned. His anger at this outrage had dissipated even more quickly than it had arisen. He looked at his daughter, trembling and sobbing, sitting hunched and frightened, like the little girl she had been for so long. He well knew that what she had done was far removed from her normal inclinations. Now, she had made it easy for him. He did not need to struggle with his conscience, nor try to reason with her, for that one act had the force of a thousand pleas. He spoke gently to her. "Tell me what you know about his medical condition." He passed her a handkerchief.

Gradually, she regained her composure and spoke again. "He's blind and deaf. It's not possible to communicate with him. When I touched his ankle he pulled a knife on me. Be warned, Daddy. He will put up a struggle". He looked into his daughters' eyes, his heart heavy with sorrow. This was the final straw. To avoid recriminations in the future he would go through with this farce. He would bring the man here, give him whatever medical help could be given, prove to Charlotte that it was not James, and then release him. When they returned to England in a few days, he would apply for psychiatric treatment for her, to release her from this self-imposed prison.

With Charlotte sitting before him, he picked up the phone. "I want an ambulance ready in five minutes, with a driver, three of your fittest men and a medic." There was a pause. "No, not a nurse, a doctor, with something to sedate an aggressive patient." He spoke to Charlotte. "Go to your quarters and stay there until I send for you. I promise I will contact you tonight." Without looking at her father, without speaking, Charlotte left the office.

Chapter 22

The driver killed the engine. The street was completely blocked by the ambulance. There was an eerie silence. "Sergeant, take a flashlight and establish if there is anyone in the room at the bottom of those steps". A few moments later the sergeant returned.

"There's a small room, sir, with a mattress on the floor and somebody on the mattress. From the size I'd say it was a man, sir."

"Right men, go in there and arrest him. You don't need to say anything to him, but he may put up a fight and he may have a weapon, but not a firearm. So, use minimum force to restrain him, and the doctor here will give him a shot to keep him quiet for a couple of hours. Carry on". The job was carried out quickly and efficiently. Within ten minutes they were en route to the base.

They carried the stretcher into the admissions room, and Sir Charles had his first view of the man's face. It *was* James. Sir Charles was to reflect, months later, that he had felt no strong emotion at all at the moment of recognition. He could remember only that he was surprise.

"Doctor, I want this man bathed and shaved. He is to have a thorough, *thorough,* medical assessment. All wounds are to be dressed, and if any surgery is required, consult me at once. If he is strong enough to undergo any vital operation I want it performed tonight. Finally, I want a full report on his condition on my desk at 8am". The doctor was fully aware of the meaning of 'thoroughly' said twice. It meant the examination had to include tests for sexually transmitted diseases.

"With respect, Sir, there is only me on duty."

Sir Charles looked at his watch. "It's only 9.30. They shouldn't be drunk yet. Send the sergeant here to find anyone you need. Carry on". The tone of his voice allowed of no further argument. He made his way to the nurses' dormitory and knocked on the door. A young nurse opened the door. Charlotte stood right behind her. Ignoring the nurse, he spoke to his daughter.   "You're right. It's him. Come to my office at 9am".

He went to the officer's mess. He gave strict instructions, through his batman, that he did not want to be approached by anyone for any purpose, except medical staff. The barman was instructed to replenish his glass whenever it was empty. The bill would be settled the following day. After an hour his presence and mood had so subdued the atmosphere that officers started to leave early. He was too immersed in his own thoughts to notice. After three hours, he was incapable of noticing anything.

Chapter 23

His solution to a hangover was always the same, and it always worked for him; sleep with the maximum amount of fresh air; arise early, whatever one's inclinations; drink as much water as possible; go for a walk; take a cold shower; and finally, to replace all the lost vitamins and minerals, eat a large English breakfast, plus some fresh fruit. By 9am he was rapidly approaching normality. The intercom buzzed. "Yes?"

"Miss Crayne is here, Sir".

"Give her a cup of tea and ask her to wait for a few minutes. I'll buzz you when I'm ready." He looked again through a summary of the medical report on James' condition;

'The patient is male, approximately 30 years of age. Name and nationality unknown. Suffering from acute bronchitis; numerous cuts and abrasions, none gangrenous; severely malnourished; there is evidence of previous frostbite; the patient does not, repeat, not, have venereal disease. N.B. eyes and tongue have been severely burned, and the eardrums punctured. The nature of these injuries suggests that the patient has been severely tortured. In all cases it seems that the damage is irreparable."

A grim frown covered Sir Charles' face. "Send in Miss Crayne".

"Daddy, I'm sorry for what I did yesterday".

"And I'm sorry for what I have been telling you for the last year, but I did it..."

"I know." Her tone permitted no further discussion on this subject. She had forgiven him for this; the matter was now closed.

"I have here a medical report, and a summary in layman's language. The summary faithfully reproduces the report. Do you want to read it?"

She could tell from his manner that it would make unpleasant reading. "Yes". He watched her as she read. It took just a few minutes to read it twice. She looked at her father, her face pale and drawn. "When can I see him?"

"They'll be changing his dressings at midday. I suggest you leave it until 1o'clock".

Chapter 24

So much information, so confusing at first. He tried to take stock, to collate the information, and come to a rational conclusion. He had been shaved, and he felt clean. The bed was warm and comfortable. There had been stinging in various parts of his body, like antiseptic applied to an open wound, but the discomfort had quickly subsided. There were bandages and sticking plaster, safety pins, and the smell of ether. Small, soft hands had touched him, feeding, wiping, tending him. Clearly, he was in a hospital. But whose hospital? British? American? Russian? God forbid, German? They had brought him a hot sweet liquid to drink. There was none of the bitter after taste associated with coffee; it was probably tea, which made it 90% certain that it was a British hospital. Still, he did nothing, revealed nothing. Once information had been given it could not be taken back. He wanted to be certain that he was safe before revealing anything about his identity.

There was movement around the bed. Someone had sat down carefully. A nurse? doctor? Soft hands touched him. A woman. She took one of his pillows and gently laid it on top of his legs. She took his right hand and carefully closed his fingers, except for the index finger. Now, using his finger, she traced two shapes on the pillow. Two circles. His furrowed brow showed her that he was confused. Again and again she drew the same pattern. Two circles. Two circles? The letter O twice? No. Not O. It was C. She was tracing C.C. There was only one other person in the world who would know the significance of these letters, this pattern. Only one other person would immediately know that this was Charlotte's initials. He tried to speak her name. She recognized the strangled cry, and tenderly squeezed his hand. He wept as they embraced. She kissed him and wiped away his tears. She held him, still sobbing, in her arms until his stressed body relaxed.

Chapter 25

James did not know how long it had been. Certainly, his wounds had healed and his health was much improved. He knew that one Christmas had passed since his rescue and he had been able to detect changes in the seasons. At this precise moment he knew what the exact date was. He was seated, outdoors, and the front of his body was hot, whereas the back of his legs and his neck were cold. He could smell the aroma of baking potatoes and treacle. It was 5th November, bonfire night, when children all over Britain celebrate the failure of a plot to blow up Parliament on this date in 1605. One of the conspirators in the plot, Guido Fawkes, was prosecuted for the offence, and each year, Guy Fawkes night is accompanied by the burning of an effigy of the unfortunate criminal, and the consumption of baked potatoes and treacle by the children. Whenever possible, fireworks are also a part of the event, but James suspected that these were a luxury too far in these times of shortage.

His mind went back to the event several years earlier when he had rescued a young girl who had ventured too close to the flames. Her dress had caught fire, but he was on hand, by pure luck, to extinguish the flames before any bodily damage could be caused. He wondered now whether the circumstances might recur on this night; he wondered if there was a young child screaming in pain, only a few feet away from him, with him the nearest adult; he cursed the fact that he would be completely unable to help. He cursed his condition, his impotence, his uselessness. Charlotte was nearby, he was quite sure of that. She came to him every few minutes, and touched his hand, exactly as they had become accustomed to, so that he would know she was there. Sometimes, Sir Charles touched his hand in his own way, different from Charlotte, unique to Sir Charles. And the same system applied to Simon, so that, at least, James knew *who* was there.

So it had been since a few days after his discharge from hospital, a dark, silent lifetime ago; tactile conversations, with 'hello', and 'goodbye', and 'I'm here' as the only content. He was glad that Simon was here tonight, because there was something between them that had to be addressed urgently. Charlotte tugged his arm gently. It was time to go indoors. James wanted to refuse, to insist on staying here, to assert himself. But what would be the point. It would only upset Charlotte, and nothing would be achieved, except the dubious proposition that he was, actually, an independent man. What a joke that would be. So now, they would go to the drawing room, and sit there, and share, he presumed, a hot, milky drink. After a while, maybe an hour, she would take him upstairs and help him to bed. She would kiss him, and embrace him, but they would not make love. Every attempt had ended in humiliating failure. He believed there would be no further activity in that area of life, ever.

Once inside the house, James indicated that he wanted to go directly to his room. There, he wrote a note asking that Simon come to him, alone. A few minutes later he felt a hand on his shoulder, Simon's agreed introduction. James led him to the dressing table and they sat down, James holding Simon's hand. He took his pencil and notepad and wrote the words 'our pledge'. Simon's blood ran cold as he remembered the night, early in the war, when the two brothers had spent an evening in a local pub. They had drunk too much, and had agreed that, if either sustained crippling injuries, the other would provide the means for suicide. It had seemed a matter of no consequence at the time, but the following morning, they had seriously and solemnly reiterated the pledge, and again several times during the following few years. James had supplied a captured revolver, with ammunition, and Simon had kept this, secretly, at his flat in London. Simon took James' hand and held it against his head, so that he could detect the shaking of his head. He had refused, broken his pledge. James, in despair at this further theft of his power to determine his own affairs, grasped Simon by the lapels. Both men stood up. James bellowed words, largely incomprehensible, but which could only be 'our pledge'!

It was the first time Simon had experienced such an atmosphere between them. James felt the anger of the betrayed; Simon, the guilt of the betrayer. He put his hands on top of James' shoulders, a conciliatory gesture. They sat down. Simon struggled with his conscience, trying to imagine the life James had lead over the last several months. He had noticed the mood swings, the growing frustration, the hopelessness that he had experienced would endure, endlessly.   Finally, James wrote another note. 'It will be my decision alone, taken calmly, without fear, whether life is worth living. I ask only that you fulfil your pledge, made solemnly, as you know I would if things were different'. It was clear enough, and it was James' right.

Two days later, Simon turned up unexpectedly at Bishops' Lodge for a brief visit, as he was 'just passing'. He carried a small case, containing the revolver and four rounds of ammunition. Unknown to anyone else, James took possession of the lethal cargo.

Chapter 26

Sir Charles walked out of the drawing room, closing the door behind him. Moments like this always made him feel sad. He remembered how, years ago on the day she had moved into his home at Bishops' Lodge, he and his new wife had resolved to redecorate the interior every seventh year. In those romantically charged days it had seemed a token of their enduring love, a renewal of their vows. He had adored her, and the memories still burned strongly in his heart. He wanted to comply with her wishes, even now, six years after her death. He had not had the work carried out during the war years as he felt it would not be proper; some people had lost their homes and all their possessions. He was sure she would understand.

Now, the war was over and things were beginning to move back to more normal conditions. He was determined that the drawing room would be finished before the end of 1947. He had inspected the preparatory work carried out by the decorators and was satisfied that all was in order. Needless to say, the room was out of bounds for the time being because of the profusion of scaffolding and the various paraphernalia of the decorator's trade.

He had always allowed his wife to choose the color schemes and textiles, because he believed that, for a woman more so than for a man, her home was a part of her very being. For her part she had always chosen wisely, acknowledging that Bishops Lodge was his home also, so that, although the decor and ambiance of each room reflected her own style and beauty and elegance, there was nowhere that made him feel less than entirely welcome and at ease.

This year he had asked Charlotte to choose the colors and materials. She had shown the same sensitivity as her mother, in spite of the fact that all materials were in short supply, and that she had been very busy helping to organize the pre-Christmas festival. This function was held each year in mid-December to raise funds for the children of the less well off. Several of the villages in the county joined in the effort, and each village staged the event as and when their turn fell due. This year it was the responsibility of the parish of Bramall Moor, in which Sir Charles' estate was located. He heard Charlotte put down the phone and walk towards the library, where he was reading the newspaper. This was going to be bad news, he was certain of that; he had noticed the intonation of her voice during the conversation. She burst into the room. "Daddy, Betty can't house sit tonight." There was near panic in her voice. 'House sitting' was the euphemism they used for protecting James in their absence. He had expressed the wish to be excluded from social events, which were not pleasurable to him, and, he presumed, burdensome to Charlotte and Sir Charles. They did not like to leave him alone and were usually fortunate enough to find someone who could be in the house if ever they both had to be away at the same time. "So, I won't be able to attend tonight." "That's a pity, but what must be must be." He was disappointed, but the safety of James was of paramount importance. There was a knock at the door. It was the vicar.

"Good afternoon, Sir Charles, Miss Charlotte. I've called around in person to talk to you about some changes we may need to make to tonight's arrangements. A number of the guests from the more distant villages have been in touch and expressed a desire that the commencement be put back slightly. Apparently, there are still difficulties getting out of London for those who work there, and they can't guarantee their arrival at the agreed time. As you and miss Charlotte are to open the proceedings it depends on whether it would cause you any inconvenience to make your opening speech at 7.30 instead of 7 o' clock".

Clearly, this would be no inconvenience, and this was merely a courtesy visit. "That would be no problem at all, but there is another problem. We have not been able to find someone to be here tonight to look after James in our absence, and my daughter is reluctant to leave him here alone."

"I see. Oh dear, it would be very disappointing if Miss Charlotte were not to attend. Very disappointing indeed." He was thoughtful for a few moments, then he continued. "Perhaps I might be able to suggest something to resolve this problem. We expect the event to last for about four hours. If I were able to arrange for one of the lady parishioners to visit James every hour or so to see that everything is in order, would that be satisfactory? I would, of course, choose someone of responsibility and trustworthiness".

"Do you have anyone in particular in mind," asked Charlotte.

"Yes. My daughter, Elizabeth."

Charlotte knew Elizabeth quite well. They had often spoken at local functions and at Church, and she had complete confidence in the younger woman. She also knew James and the geography of Bishops' Lodge. She would be the ideal choice. "Wouldn't she want to spend all her time at the fete?"

"I'm sure she wouldn't mind popping out every hour or so in the circumstances. It's only three miles to the Church Hall, and she has her little car. Each visit would take less than half an hour."

"Fine. That's settled then. We'll be there shortly after 7."

"Thank you very much." The vicar took his leave.

Chapter 27

Tomato soup, roast chicken and apple pie. It had been one of his favorite meals when he was a man. He imagined this was why Charlotte had prepared it. He could tell what it was from the aromas, but he could taste hardly anything. It was as if the food mocked him. He wondered if people mocked him. Not Charlotte and Sir Charles, of course, because they loved him. They would not mock him. They would pity him.

Probably, most people would not mock his actual afflictions, but some would certainly laugh at the results, his awkwardness and clumsiness. He was sure of one thing; no-one would mock his clothes; odd socks or shoes, trousers and shirts of ridiculous colors. No possibility of that, because every day Charlotte laid out the clothes he was to wear. Once he had refused to wear the clothes she had presented, throwing them across the room. She had given him other clothes, or perhaps the same clothes. How could he know? She had not remonstrated with him for this tantrum. Perhaps she understood his frustration. It was nice when people understood. It was nice when they knew what it was like to be hopeless and helpless and useless.

Here she was again, tugging his arm gently, so gently. Must not do anything dangerous or likely to alarm him. All must be soft and gentle and kind, as you would treat a child. It must be time to go for afternoon coffee, but this time in the lounge, not the drawing room as usual. But why not the drawing room? He would like to know. Just once he would like to be consulted, to decide for himself. But how? How could they ask him anything? Or explain anything? She led him to one of the ropes which had been fixed all around the house so that he could find his way by touch. He grasped the rope and wrenched his arm from her grip. He wondered what color the rope was, how the house looked with rope everywhere. Like a boxing ring? Like a prison? A prison for Charlotte! What a pity! She should complain! Some people had worse prisons, like their own body. They had all let him down, all of them. Simon had tried to let him down, but he was so weak that even a shell of a man, like James, could impose his will. He had gone against a vicious enemy to save them all, and they had all let him down. Sir Charles had told him Stockhausen was dead. What a laugh! Charlotte's wonderful magic had not helped him; Simon's triumphant air force; Henri's Resistance; the men he had trained and fought with; all had failed him in the most critical hour of his life. Now, they kept him, like a pet, to ease their consciences. They could all go to Hell!

Chapter 28

It had only just dawned on him that he was alone. Certainly, shortly after dinner, she had tried to convey something, some information, but it had all been gibberish. So, he nodded his head as if he understood, and she ceased her nonsense and left him. Later, he had clapped his hands, the signal that he wanted something. No-one had come to him. So, he was alone. Good. He did not want her here. She was as much use to him as he was to her.

He sat, silent, brooding and bitter, unaware that the vicar's daughter stood at the door, watching him. He was unaware, also, of her departure. After a few moments, he stood up. He had had a good idea. He would go around the house, go into every room, just to do it on his own initiative, by his own authority.

He slammed the lounge door twice. The noise did not grate on his nerves, for he could not hear it. There could be no stresses in his life; the sun was never too bright for his eyes; food never too sweet or bitter; the crying of children never assailed him. He approached the drawing room. The door was locked, but the key had been left in the lock. He turned the key and entered the room. Immediately, he noticed the aroma of some chemical which he could not recognize, even though he knew he had smelt it before. They must have done a deep clean in this room recently. Very commendable! They must have locked the door so that he could not get in and untidy things. He left the door ajar. He reached for the rope. It was gone. Perhaps their idea of a joke, or perhaps he was to be denied access to certain rooms from now on. Well, it was their house and they could do what they wanted! They could put him in the cellar if they liked! In fact, he would prefer that, to get away from their hypocrisy!

He assumed the drawing room would be in its normal condition, as he had last seen it, a lifetime ago. The thick, heavy curtains would be drawn across the window at the front of the room; the large settee and the armchairs would be grouped around the fireplace. At the rear of the room, opposite the large window, would be the built-in bookcase resplendent with the collection of books built up by the Crayne family over three generations. Next to the fireplace would be the writing bureau, and on top of that would be the wireless. Several small coffee tables and footstools would be spread around at various points. He took a step forward and tripped over a dismantled trestle table.

It was boring, but Charlotte would make the best of it. The woman was repeating the same stories, with slight variations where she had forgotten previous embellishments. The men were inventing stories about their conquests, of all types, during the war. She had seen the vicar's daughter return from her hourly visit to Bishops Lodge and had acknowledged her smile of reassurance. She looked over to where her father stood, in the center of a group of older men. She alone in the room noticed him raise his eyes to the ceiling. They exchanged a knowing smile. She knew he would listen patiently, saying little of his role in the armed forces. To do so would diminish most of those around him. Turning back to the group of women, she felt a sudden, momentary, surge of unease. She looked at the vicar's daughter. She was chatting happily to a young man.

James picked himself up, sullenly, and stepped backwards. His face touched the cold steel of a scaffold tube. His body became rigid. It was the barrel of a revolver. From the corner of his eye he could see the grinning oafish face of Stein. He saw the single light bulb burning above the interrogation table. Stein spoke. "Move" His voice was distant, jarring, almost non-human. James walked forward and fell over an unseen obstruction. The temple of his head was gashed against some sharp object. Warm, sticky blood seeped down his face. He heard laughter; mocking girlish laughter. Looking up, he saw Gisela. As he stood up, Stein smashed the revolver onto the back of his head. The scaffold shook under the impact. James looked up and saw Stockhausen sitting at the table. He launched himself at his arch enemy and sent his fist crashing into Stockhausen's face, but he moved too quickly, and James' fist smashed into the wall, breaking his middle and ring fingers.

"And she expects to go back into teaching as soon as..." It was a polite conversation, small talk, but Charlotte did not respond. A feeling of nausea overwhelmed her. Without a word she rushed from the Hall to her car. It was three miles home; ten minutes. She would do it in eight.

James knelt on the floor of the cell, nursing his broken hand, breathing heavily. Now, there was laughter all around, echoing off the walls. Sir Charles was sitting on the top step, kissing Gisela. Stockhausen was leaning against a wall, his arm around Charlotte's shoulder. They were both laughing, Charlotte's face distorted, cruel. Stockhausen's hand covered her breast; she emitted a raucous, hollow cackle. Enraged, James charged across the room, woefully gashing his shin against another unseen obstruction. His hands closed around Stockhausen's throat, thin, cold and metallic. He began to throttle his tormentor, but still Stockhausen laughed. James shook him from side to side. He was knocked unconscious when the scaffolding collapsed on him.

Charlotte's heart sank when she saw James. Slowly, carefully, she began to remove the steel tubes which pinned him to the floor.

Chapter 30

It was Karin, he was sure. She had come for him again, to take him home, to reclaim him. He felt her small body tremble under the burden of his weight as she helped him up the steps. She guided him to the bed where she helped him to lay down. She wiped his face with a soft, damp cloth. Slowly, he began to recover. She took his hand and squeezed it in a certain way. He recognized a signal, but he was confused. Now she was making other signs; still, confusion. She left him alone. He explored his surroundings; a large bed, with blankets and pillows. This was not Karin's home. Then he knew. This was Bishops' Lodge. Even Karin had played a trick on him, a cruel heartless deception. Well, there would be no more.

Charlotte had left him on the bed, resting. Her nerves were taut and strained, she was consumed by guilt as she went to the kitchen. She would give him a brandy, and then a cup of tea, that great standby of the British. This would help for the moment, but in the long run, there were problems which would require professional help. She could sense his frustration, but was powerless to help, and yet, despite all this, she knew that she still loved him deeply. For James, she realized, life must be a nightmare. She looked at her reflection in the mirror. The strain showed.

Suddenly, she heard an explosive sound, like the crack of a whip, from
somewhere inside the house. It resounded in her head, blasting through her, vibrating the very fibers of her body. Adrenalin poured into her bloodstream as she realized what the sound was. It was the report of a pistol being fired.

The End